Praise for *Head of the Snake*

Gary Quesenberry's *Head of the Snake* hits with the speed and precision of a close-quarters strike. This isn't just another thriller—it's a hard-edged, deeply human story about duty, loss, and the scars we carry long after the fight. Case Younger is the kind of man you want on your six—a warrior forged by pain and sharpened by purpose. Quesenberry gets the tactics right, but more importantly, he gets the people right. Fans of authentic, boots-on-the-ground storytelling—this one's for you.
 —Alan C. Mack, U.S. Army CW5 Retired, author of *Razor 03, A Night Stalker's Wars*

Gary Quesenberry's *Head of the Snake* stands in a league of its own. The action is raw, the details are spot-on, and the story grabs you by the throat from page one. Quesenberry brings a level of realism and intensity that only someone who's truly been there can deliver. *Head of the Snake* is a hard-hitting, no-BS conclusion to one of the best thriller series I've read in years.
 —Phil Morden, former Navy SEAL and owner of Element Epic Entertainment

Gary Quesenberry has done it again. His new novel, *Head of the Snake,* proves he has what it takes to compete with "The Bigs" in the world of thriller fiction. Simply put: Case Younger kicks ass!
 —Dave Temple, host of The Thriller Zone podcast

Head of the Snake is packed with relentless action in a perfect mix of military operations, crime thrills, and adrenaline rushes swirling in a wildly gripping story of shadowy play-for-keeps stakes that will dare readers to put it down. Case Younger is at his best when the stakes are higher than ever.
—Jeff Clark, US Air Force (Retired), author of *Hear These Truths: The Ultimate Guide to Building Your Leadership Algorithm,* host of the Course of Action podcast

Gary Quesenberry's *Head of the Snake* is a fantastic and fitting conclusion to the Case Younger trilogy, picking up right after the events that began with the incredibly suspenseful *Homecoming* and then continued with edge-of-your-seat intensity in *Dead to Rights.*

I won't give anything away, but here's what I can tell you. *Head of the Snake* does not disappoint. The suspense, tension, and danger are present from the first chapter and never let up. Since the events of *Homecoming*, our hero, former U.S. Air Marshal, Case Younger, has wanted to find a little bit of peace and quiet in his hometown of Pikesville, VA. But that peace is hard fought as Younger is plunged deeper and deeper into a dark web of conspiracy, corruption, and with a high price on his head.

The twists and turns are inspired. The tension is palpable, and the danger…nonstop.

While I sincerely hope that Case Younger gets pulled into more adventures in future novels, *Head of the Snake,* like the first two in this "hard to put down" Case Younger trilogy, is a fantastic read, and one I'll be telling all my friends about. I highly recommend!
—Jude Gerard Prest, executive producer of *Titan: The Ocean Gate Disaster* / CEO-showrunner-director-writer: LifeLike Productions, Inc.

Gary Quesenberry's *Head of the Snake* is a hard-hitting follow-up to *Dead to Rights,* completing the Case Younger trilogy. Quesenberry's writing shines through with layered characters that more than feel real, over the trilogy, they've become family. That's the joy of the Case Younger trilogy—more than pulse-pounding action and a former practitioner's authenticity—it's the deep sense of honor and heart that Quesenberry imbues in his characters. His blend of diving action and emotion will resonate with readers of Ryan Steck's *Matthew Redd* saga. Gripping and immersive, Gary Quesenberry is one to watch.
—Delbert Roll, MAJ (Ret), United States Army, CIA Operations Officer (Ret). Author of *Lessons in Professional Relationship Management from a CIA Operations Officer*

I picked up *Head of the Snake* without reading the previous two books in the series, but it didn't matter. Gary Quesenberry effortlessly provided all the backstory I needed while launching me into Case Younger's latest adventure, one filled with real characters you actually care about. Including an aging hitman whose love of his pet cat and budding romance with a local coffee-shop waitress made me want an entire book about him, even though he's ostensibly one of the "bad guys." This is good stuff, folks.
—Gregg Podolski, author of *The Recruiter*

HEAD OF THE SNAKE

Nonfiction books by Gary Quesenberry:

Spotting Danger Before It Spots You
Spotting Danger Before It Spots Your Kids
Spotting Danger Before It Spots Your Teens
Spotting Danger for Travelers

Fiction by Gary Quesenberry:

Homecoming
Dead to Rights

Head of the Snake

A CASE YOUNGER THRILLER

GARY QUESENBERRY

YMAA Publication Center
Wolfeboro, NH USA

YMAA Publication Center, Inc.
PO Box 480
Wolfeboro, NH 03894
1-800-669-8892 • www.ymaa.com • info@ymaa.com

ISBN 9781594390746 (print)
ISBN 9781594390791 (hardcover)
ISBN 9781594391033 (ebook)

© 2026 by Gary Quesenberry
All rights reserved including the right of reproduction in whole or in part in any form. Any use of this intellectual property for text and data mining or computational analysis including as training material for artificial intelligence systems is strictly prohibited without express written consent. For permission requests, contact the Publisher.

Edited by: Leslie Takao
Cover Design: Axie Breen

20260206

Publisher's Cataloging in Publication

Names: Quesenberry, Gary, author.

Title: Head of the snake : a Case Younger thriller / Gary Quesenberry.

Description: Wolfeboro, NH USA : YMAA Publication Center, [2026] | Sequel to the author's "Homecoming" and "Dead to Rights".

Identifiers: LCCN: 2026931839 | ISBN: 9781594390746 (print) | 9781594390791 (hardcover) | 9781594391033 (ebook)

Subjects: LCSH: Home--United States--Fiction. | Friendship--Fiction. | Human trafficking--Fiction. | Political corruption--Fiction. | Assassins--Fiction. | Justice--Fiction. | Family secrets--Fiction. | Redemption--Fiction. | Suspense fiction. | LCGFT: Thrillers (Fiction) | Detective and mystery fiction. | Action and adventure fiction. | BISAC: FICTION / Thrillers / Crime. | FICTION / Mystery & Detective / Hard-Boiled. | FICTION / Small Town & Rural.

Classification: LCC: PS3617.U48 H43 2026 | DDC: 813/.6--dc23

This is a work of fiction. Names, characters, places, and incidents either are the product of the author's imagination or are used fictitiously, and any resemblance to actual persons, living or dead, businesses, companies, events, or locales is entirely coincidental.

Printed in USA.

This one's for you Mom.

The woods are lovely, dark and deep.
But I have promises to keep,
And miles to go before I sleep,
And miles to go before I sleep.

—*Robert Frost*

PROLOGUE
Richmond, Virginia
1982

Jack was drinking again. It had started a week ago and was progressively getting worse. It always began the same way—just a beer or two after work with his friends. Then he'd move on to the hard stuff and spiral into a two-week bender. His live-in girlfriend, Vera, caught the overpowering stench of bourbon and cheap perfume on him as soon as he walked in the door that evening, but she knew better than to bring it up. Now, it was just a matter of time. He stomped through the house, ranting and raving, searching for an excuse to leave. Vera tried to melt into the background. She knew that once he found something to provoke a reaction, he'd beat her senseless and walk out, leaving her to tend to the twins alone.

Jack stood in the center of the room, shouting while Vera sat trembling on the couch, making herself as small as possible. That's when the babies started to cry.

"Jesus fucking Christ! Have you even fed those two today?"

"Of course I have, Jack," Vera said timidly, "They're just crying because you—"

That was all the excuse he needed. Jack clenched his fists and charged toward Vera,

"Because I what?" He spat, hovering over the cowering woman.

Vera knew she was about to take another beating, so what the hell. She might as well fight back. "Because you started yelling, Jack." She screamed, standing to face her tormentor, her own hands now balled tightly into fists. "I've been here all day caring for these babies, doing your laundry, and keeping your house clean. And what do I get in return? A man who comes home smelling like a god damned—"

The first punch caught her full in the face, sending her crashing to the floor. Then the kicking started. Vera curled herself into the fetal position and pressed her back against the couch to protect her spine. She covered her head, neck, and ribs with her arms—a defensive technique she'd perfected over time. Vera would stay this way until Jack wore himself out, which didn't take long. After a few seconds of kicking and stomping, the drunkard stopped and put his hands on his knees, heaving for breath.

"You're a shit mother, you know that?"

Vera stayed silent on the floor, feeling little drops of blood trickle from the wounds on her shins and forearms.

"And I know one of these days, that little girl in there is gonna be a shit mother too."

Jack stood up straight and walked into the bedroom. When he returned, he was carrying an old navy sea bag and one of the twins wrapped in a light blue blanket.

"But there's no way in hell I'm gonna let you ruin my boy."

"Jack, no...Please," Vera begged as she struggled to her knees.

"You do whatever you want with that little bitch in there. But this one belongs to me."

Without looking back, Jack grabbed his coat and walked out the door with his son in his arms, leaving Vera crying on her knees and little baby Tina screaming in the next room.

It had been five days, and Jack still hadn't come home. He usually stayed gone when he was like this, but he'd never left with one of the children before. Vera was terrified. She called everyone she knew to ask if they'd seen Jack around town, but no one had. She drove to all the bars and strip clubs he frequented when he was drinking, but again, no one had heard from the man. Finally, after a month of waiting and searching, Vera resigned herself to the truth—Jack was never coming back, and despite the possibility that she might never see her son again, she felt a sense of relief.

Vera stood at the dresser and looked in the mirror. Her eyes were clear, and her face was free of bruises. She'd been sleeping at night—not the fitful, restless sleep of a woman in fear, but a deep, peaceful slumber she hadn't known in years. She glanced past her reflection to see the packed suitcase lying on the bed and little Tina resting quietly in her carrier. She was reluctant to leave. She knew that once she walked out the door, she'd never come back, even if it meant losing her baby boy. The way Vera saw it, she could either stay and risk Jack destroying them all or leave and at least save little Tina. The two of them could have a better life somewhere new, free from the yoke of a man like Jack.

Vera turned and sat on the edge of the bed. She pulled down the soft satin blanket that covered Tina and kissed the untamed waves of thick black curls atop her head. The baby smiled and kicked excitedly. She was happy.

"It's just me and you now, sweet girl. But I promise, I'll never let a man like that around you again. I will erase that memory from our lives so we can start over and you can have the life you deserve. How does that sound?"

Tina babbled incoherently and stretched her tiny arms

toward her mother. That was all the validation Vera needed. She grabbed her suitcase and the baby and packed them safely in the station wagon her friend Nancy had loaned her, along with a box that held her most cherished possessions—her mother's rose-pattern tea set, and the Scott family bible. Vera sat pensively in the driveway as the car idled, looking at an overgrown yard and a house that had never felt any real love. *Never again*, she promised herself, and with a renewed spirit, Vera shifted the station wagon into reverse, backed slowly out of the driveway, and headed south toward the only place she'd ever been happy—her grandmother's old homeplace in the quiet little town of Pikesville, Virginia.

Part One
Escalation

Chapter 1
Present Day

August Moody woke to the sound of breaking glass. His ash-gray eyes opened slowly but showed no signs of panic or alarm. At fifty-nine years old, he'd been in his fair share of bad situations, so instead of grabbing for the phone to call the police, he grabbed for the heavy steel-framed Sig P226 sitting on his nightstand, performed a low-light press check, and shuffled calmly toward the door.

August had lived in the same house for almost five years now—longer than he'd ever stayed in any one place, and it had unexpectedly started to feel like home. The small, two-story Victorian sat on the western corner of South Bell and 110th Street in the Beverly district of South Chicago, across from a quaint little coffee shop that August visited most mornings. Maria worked there. She was close to his age and, aside from his business contacts, was the only person, in too long a while, he'd had an actual conversation with. She was sweet and always greeted him with a smile. He'd even go so far as to say he liked her. Hell, he liked the whole neighborhood. It was clean and quiet, and everyone tended to mind their own business. It was a place where August could see himself growing old and perhaps even making a few friends. It wasn't that he never wanted friends, but given the nature of his job, relationships of any kind didn't seem particularly smart, so he stayed away from them. Hopefully, that would all change now that he was thinking of retirement. Maybe then he could even ask Maria out to dinner.

August stood at the edge of the door frame and slowly

pushed his head out into the darkness. He looked left, then right, before taking three quick steps forward and glancing over the railing that hung above the hallway downstairs. There were no signs of movement, no flashlights swinging wildly through the night, no sound, just silence. August crept toward the staircase and started downward, carefully keeping his weight close to the edges so the steps didn't creak. Once at the bottom, he raised his pistol and swung left into the dining room. There was nothing there, so he continued cautiously down the hallway.

Further along, he came to the wide, arched opening that led into the kitchen and the back entryway. August reached his hand around to the light switch on the opposing wall and quickly flipped it up. He sidestepped right, gun up and searching as his eyes adjusted to the brightness. It only took a second for him to acquire his target.

"DJ," August yelled as his pistol swept across the cat sitting on the edge of the sink, looking amusedly at the broken drinking glass scattered across the hardwood floor below. August let out a sigh and relaxed. "Bad cat."

Exasperated, he set his pistol on the countertop, walked over to the black and gold tortie shorthair, grabbed her softly by the face, and looked her in the eyes. They reminded him of large yellow diamonds, bright and shimmering.

"What's the matter, huh? Do I not give you enough attention?"

August picked up DJ and stroked her gently. He'd had the cat for as long as he'd lived in the house. He found her in the small shed out back when she was just a timid and slightly malnourished kitten. August had brought her inside, fed her, and taken her to the vet for shots and a checkup. Now, she had the run of the house and always found ways to keep August on his toes. He lovingly set her back on the counter and patted her head.

"Now, you stay here. I'll clean this mess up so we can go back to bed, okay?"

After sweeping up the broken glass and tossing it in the trash can, August retrieved his pistol and the cat, flipped the kitchen light off, and carried the purring feline with him as he headed back to his room.

"You're gonna stay with me tonight so you don't get into any more mischief, understand?"

As August approached the stairs, he noticed a faint blinking light coming from the study to his left, indicating that he had a message waiting on his computer.

August huffed, "Okay, DJ. It looks like I have to go to work," he said as he dropped the cat onto the hall rug. "No more trouble tonight. I mean it." He admonished as DJ sprinted back toward the kitchen, trailed by the faint jingling of the small bell on her collar.

August walked into the study, sat at his antique French mahogany desk, and opened his laptop to find a message addressed to Mr. White, his primary alias. It was from Senator Glen Whitlock.

Mr. White,
Cleanup needed down south: The mess is bigger than usual, so I'm adjusting your pay accordingly: 150 up front, 150 after. See attached.

Three hundred thousand—must be a big one. August was intrigued, so he double-clicked on the attachment and waited for the decryption software to do its job. After a few seconds, his laptop screen was filled with photos, addresses, descriptions, and a list of instructions. He recognized the man in the images. His face had been plastered all over the news about a year ago. He and several other air marshals had stopped a hijacking over Paris, France, potentially saving thousands of lives in the process. He was considered a national hero but had dropped out of public view since the incident occurred. August stared at the man's icy blue eyes and read the description.

Name: Case Younger
Age: 42 years old
Height: 6'1"
Weight: 195 pounds
Residence: Pikesville, Virginia
Task: Kill. No capture.
Notes: Former Army Ranger and counter-terror operative. Multiple combat deployments. Highly skilled in firearms, tactics, hand-to-hand combat, explosives, improvised weapons, and escape and evasion.
Extreme caution required.

August was surprised that someone would want a man like Case Younger dead, but that was of no concern to him. Work was work. Still, given the target's background, this wouldn't be an easy job like some of the other unsuspecting troublemakers he'd taken down in the past. Younger would be hard to kill. If he were going to do this right, he'd need some help. August dragged his cursor over to the secure email app and opened it.

Joe,
I need assistance with a job. Meet me in Charlotte, NC—the day after tomorrow. Enterprise car rental.
AM

After hitting send, August sat back in his chair and folded his arms. He'd been a paid killer for a very long time. He had a knack for it and, over the years, had established a reputation for efficiency and discretion among a handful of very wealthy and influential clients, Senator Whitlock being one of them. But this was it. He was getting too old for this shit and needed a change in his life. He was ready for it—hell, he deserved it after everything he'd done for these people. In this business, death was always close, and August knew better than to push his luck. Case Younger would be the last man he ever killed for money.

Chapter 2

Case Younger stood in the barn, struggling under the weight of the fiberglass camper top he was installing on his dad's 1976 Dodge Power Wagon. The old topper had been sitting under a tarp for ages and looked a bit worse for wear. Case held fond memories of his dad loading the camper up in late summer to take him and his little brother Bobby on weekend trips to Hanging Rock. It was big and cumbersome, and if it hadn't been for the help of his friend and neighbor, Dimpsey Campbell, he wouldn't have bothered with it at all.

"You gonna be okay over there?" Dimpsey asked with a chuckle as he waited for Case to find the grip he needed on his side of the camper.

Since childhood, Case had always been impressed with the older man's strength. Even now, in his seventies, Dimpsey could still lift more weight than someone half his age—the result of a lifetime spent working on a farm.

"I'll be just fine over here. Now, sit your end up on the bed, and I'll—"

Before Case could finish his sentence, Dimpsey heaved his side of the camper top into the truck bed and walked around to help.

"Let me give ya a hand here, pal," Dimpsey said, looking sympathetically at Case,

"Smartass." Case grumbled under his breath as he shifted the camper into its final position and shook the fatigue from his arms. "I could have gotten it myself."

Dimpsey laughed. "I never doubted it. It just looked like you could use an extra set of hands, is all."

Case ignored the comment and changed the subject. "Speaking of extra hands, where's Trevor been lately? I haven't seen him around much since the incident with Wilks and his crew."

Dimpsey's grandson, Trevor, had been through a lot over the past several days. He'd been held hostage and used as a human shield by a man named JC Wilks, who was part of the Dead Rebels Motorcycle Club. The gang was out for revenge against Case for dismantling their human trafficking operation and Trevor had quite literally been caught in the crossfire. The whole situation had been a complete mess. The only good thing to come from it was discovering the identity of the person behind it all. Now, Case was preparing to link up with his former colleagues on the Critical Missions Project in McLean, Virginia, to apprehend the man responsible—a wealthy real estate investor by the name of Tanner Greene.

"I know this hasn't been easy on the boy, but it's not like him to be so dang quiet," Dimpsey responded.

"It's certainly a change. But give him some time. He's just gotta process things in his own way. You know how that is."

The old veteran nodded solemnly and turned when he noticed someone walking through the open barn door. It was Case's girlfriend, Sam. She was carrying a large serving tray full of sandwiches and a big pitcher of freshly squeezed lemonade.

"I thought you boys could use some lunch before I leave for work. You got everything situated for the trip?" She asked, looking at Case while Dimpsey eagerly grabbed a sandwich from the tray.

"Just about. We still need to clamp the camper top on the

truck bed, then I'll re-caulk the windows. That should help protect my gear during the drive."

"Do you know when you'll be leaving yet?" Sam asked.

"Matt and Ross are up north putting together the target package. I'll leave as soon as they let me know they're ready."

"I'm still not convinced you going along is a good idea," Dimpsey interjected between mouthfuls of ham and cheese.

"I started this mess when I took on the Dead Rebels. Now, I aim to see it finished for good." Case responded a little more forcefully than he meant to.

"He's right, Dimpsey. This needs to end." Sam added. "I'm just glad you're doin' it right and not goin' at this alone like you did in Richmond."

Case hung his head. He'd always had a temper. It was a sinister trait that he'd inherited from his father, and he had worked hard to keep it under control, but not always successfully. He'd lost it when Rex Kelley and his gang kidnapped Sam's daughter, Mia, almost a year ago. Their plan was to sell her into the trafficking stream to repay some debts. Case followed the club back to their headquarters in Richmond and killed most of the Dead Rebels' chain of command. Only JC Wilks had survived.

"Well, it's still dangerous." Dimpsey responded.

"It is. But this time, I have the full backing of the Joint Task Force and the CMP. It'll be an easy takedown compared to the others."

"I suppose," Dimpsey grumbled before taking a swig of his lemonade. "Anyway, let's get this camper finished up before you lose what little strength you have left."

Case laughed and shook his head, amazed at the man's stamina. Dimpsey had always been like a surrogate father to him. In fact, his dad, Avis, and Dimpsey had been best friends growing up and had served together in Vietnam. When Avis passed away, Dimpsey stepped in and took care of the farm for Case's little brother, Bobby. The man was like a member of the family, and his concern was appreciated.

Case looked back at Dimpsey and grinned, "I guess we should. I wouldn't want you to have to carry me back the house."

Trevor sat on the edge of the small walking bridge with Mia, absentmindedly pitching tiny stones into the babbling waters below his feet. The sun was high, and the breeze was light, but Trevor's mood was dark and sullen. Mia hated seeing him like this but understood why he felt the way he did.

Less than a week ago, he'd found out from one of his captors that his mother, Tina, was still alive. Trevor's father, Dimpsey's son, had died when Trevor was just a toddler, and his mom had run away with a local drug dealer shortly afterward. Trevor hadn't seen or heard from his mom since then but had always imagined she was out there somewhere—waiting for him to come find her.

"Did you talk to your grandpa yet?" Mia asked, trying to snap Trevor out of his depressive mood.

"Why? He'd just try to stop me. I don't think he ever liked my mom much anyway."

"What are you gonna do?"

Trevor thought for a moment, "I'm gonna go find her."

Mia's big brown eyes went wide. "How?"

Trevor looked over his shoulder toward the barn. Case and Dimpsey had finished with the camper and were walking back toward the house with Sam.

"I'm gonna hide in Case's truck when he leaves. It'll take most of the day to reach his buddies up north, so he won't even know I'm there till we get to McLean. Then I'll tell him what happened and ask him to help me."

"Why not just ask him now. I'm sure he'll understand."

Trevor shook his head. Everyone looked at him like he was still a child, but he knew he was capable enough to do this on his own. He just needed the proper resources, and Case's friends in the CMP would have those.

"Case is just like Grandpa. He'll tell me no flat out or at least try to talk me out of it. She's my mom, and if she's out there, I feel like she'd appreciate it if I tried to find her. I want her to know that I still love her and that it's okay. She can come back home now."

Mia put her arm around the boy she adored and kissed him on the cheek. "I understand. I'll help any way I can. But if Case figures out what you're up to, he's gonna be upset."

Trevor threw the last of his pebbles into the stream and stood. Without his baseball cap, the thick brown curls on his head danced wildly in the breeze. "I know. So, it's best he don't find out. Promise me you won't say anything."

Mia looked Trevor in the eyes. She could see he was struggling and would do whatever it took to see the boy happy again.

"Okay, Trevor. I promise."

Chapter 3
Pikesville, Virginia
1987

Vera sat on the front porch of her childhood home talking to Nancy Delaney, who'd driven down from Richmond for a visit. The women had been friends since the eighth grade and knew practically everything about each other. Both had been active in sports and counted among the popular kids in school. Nancy had been a cheerleader all the way into college, and Vera ran track, winning the district championship in the girl's 800-meter her junior and senior years.

Little Tina, who'd just turned six, and Nancy's daughter, Grace, played happily in the front yard, running around the swing set, chasing after an errant butterfly, filling the air with laughter.

"God, they've grown so much in the last five years," Nancy noted.

"Yes, they have."

Nancy looked over at Vera and, for the first time in years, saw that her friend was happy.

"You look great, Vera. Settling down here has been good for you."

"It is good for me. And I know it's what Tina needed, but..." Vera stopped speaking, and the smile that had graced her lips began to fade.

"What?" Nancy pressed.

"It's nothing."

"Bullshit. Come clean."

"I just worry about my little boy. For the last five years, he's been with Jack, and I have no way of knowing how he's doing or if he's okay. It weighs on me."

Nancy put her hand on Vera's knee and looked her in the eyes, "I understand that, Vera. But that man was hurting you. He would have eventually gone too far. Then where would Tina be? You did the right thing."

"But what if he's had time to think about things? What if he's changed and realizes that he made a mistake."

The statement broke Nancy's heart. As a social worker, she'd seen and heard too many women in Vera's position talk that way—trying to justify or overlook the actions of their abusers.

"No, Vera. You can't think like that. Men like Jack don't change. If you went back now, it would just put you both in danger again."

"Maybe. I just don't want to deprive Tina of a family because I didn't do everything I could have."

Nancy shook her head. "Okay, say you go back and find Jack. What if he hasn't changed, and things go right back to how they were? Then, one day, he gets tired of beating on you and decides to turn on Tina. How could you live with yourself knowing that you put her in a position to get hurt?"

Vera watched Tina and Grace run around the tiny yard. As harsh as it sounded, she knew her friend was just being honest.

"That's not something I could live with. But one of these days, she's gonna start askin' about her daddy. What am I supposed to tell her then?"

Nancy looked out at Tina, who was now embroiled in a fierce game of tag with Grace.

"You tell her the truth. That her father was a horrible man who almost killed you, and you had to run in order to save yourself and her."

"And what do I tell her about her brother?"

Nancy sat silently, choosing her words carefully, "Why put that on her, Vera? Look at her—she's happy, healthy, and loved. Personally, I wouldn't do anything to jeopardize that. Not at her age. Let her grow up and have a normal life here in Pikesville. Then, when she's older and mature enough to understand the circumstances, maybe you can talk to her about it."

Vera thought about her life before and what it looked like now. How could she even consider going back to something that would only hurt and confuse Tina.

"You're right, Nancy. Tina is my life now, and I'll do everything I can to protect her. I'll keep the past where it belongs."

Chapter 4
Present Day

August stretched to retrieve the leather duffle he kept on the top shelf of his closet. He packed only the essentials. He assumed this job would be more complex and unpredictable than most. He didn't imagine the Younger job would take very long and would purchase whatever else he needed once he arrived in Virginia and solidified his plan. He knew that Case Younger would be hard to approach and even harder to kill, but wasn't worried. Despite the risks, August was confident that he could finish the job. That's why he was so well compensated for the work he did. August also took into account that Younger's sudden death would most certainly make the news and raise questions—questions that, if pursued, could expose Senator Whitlock and open August up to retaliation. To avoid all that, it would be imperative that this one look like an accident. That's one of the reasons he'd contacted Joe.

Joseph Seferi had worked with August on several jobs in the past, and although the two men didn't appear to have much in common, August found Joe to be competent, professional, and deadly—all critical traits in their line of work. Of the five people "Mr. White" offered his services to, Glen Whitlock was the only one who took offense to Joe. The politicians always seemed to prefer their triggermen a little older, cleaner, and more businesslike. Joe was none of those things, but he was smart and effective, and whether Whitlock liked it or not, Seferi was the man August had chosen as his successor.

DJ meowed and brushed forcefully against August's pant

leg until the man picked her up.

"What's the matter, girl? You know I'm leaving, don't you? Don't worry, I won't be gone long. Then, when I get back, I'll be back for good. I promise."

August scratched behind the cat's ears as she stretched out her neck and purred.

"In the meantime, maybe you can help me out with something."

August usually took DJ to a local kennel when he had to leave on business, but knowing this was his last job, perhaps it was time for a change.

"I'm going to walk over to the coffee shop later and talk to Maria. Maybe you can help an old man land a date. What do you think?"

DJ pressed her head against August's hand and continued purring in earnest. "That's my girl," the man said as he sat the cat gingerly on the bed and began laying out his things.

After packing, August stood in the steaming shower with his hands pressed firmly against the white tiled wall. Thin jets of hot water beat against his back. His body ached from the decades of abuse he'd subjected it to, and he contemplated the possibilities of what might lie ahead. He didn't know why he'd been so reflective lately—age, he assumed—but despite the years he'd spent working as a hired killer, maybe the rest of his life could be different. August would manage the planning and coordination of the job once they'd made it to Virginia, but he wanted Joe to handle the rest. That would be the best way for him to prove his worth to Whitlock and take over the business once August stepped aside. He knew there would be pushback, but it was his decision to make.

August turned off the water and grabbed his towel from the silver hook beside the shower door. He scrubbed the short gray stubble on his head and patted his face dry before wrapping the towel around his waist.

"Shit," he mumbled, looking down.

Either the towel was shrinking, or August was getting a little thicker around the middle. He stared critically at himself in the mirror. Despite the scarring he'd accumulated over the years and the few extra pounds, he was pleased with what he saw. Strength and endurance had always been a part of the job, so he worked hard to keep himself in shape. He was a former Marine, after all, and Marines had an image to uphold no matter how old they were.

"It has to be the towel," August laughed to himself.

After shaving and brushing his teeth, August checked himself in the mirror again and put on a pair of comfortable jeans and his favorite forest green button-up. He headed downstairs and was met at the door by DJ. August reached down and gave the cat another pat on the head.

"You stay here, Deej, I'll be right back."

August stepped out into the early morning sun and closed the door behind him as recreational joggers and clusters of women pushing baby strollers swept past, smiling. Moody smiled back politely and steadied his nerves. Killing may have come easily to him, but it had been a long time since he'd pursued a woman romantically. He was a little nervous.

Chapter 5

Matt Barrett stood in the briefing room, arranging the printouts that were scattered across the long government-issue conference table. Light fell through the tall, narrowly spaced windows, casting shadows across the collected surveillance photos of Tanner Greene. Matt picked one up and studied the man's small, condescending eyes.

What a fucking asshole. He thought before pitching the photo back onto the table and retrieving the fact sheet he'd been given by the CMP's intel division.

Tanner Greene was the founder and CEO of Stonehill Investment Group, a real estate investment company that had been on *Forbes'* Fortune 500 list for nearly a decade. Over that time, Greene had amassed a personal fortune, most of which had been earned through legal and respectable channels. Still, there was a portion of his earnings that didn't make sense until they were viewed as illicit gains—then everything clicked into place.

Matt hadn't had much experience with human trafficking until joining the Federal Air Marshal Service. Part of his FAM education involved a series of mandatory online training courses. Through those, the physical indicators of human trafficking had stuck in his mind, and on several occasions, he and his team were able to identify and apprehend traffickers moving victims through the aviation domain. As satisfying as those arrests may have been, he knew they were only part of the problem. Global profits from human trafficking exceeded two hundred and thirty billion dollars annually, and the men who benefited the most from it always managed to stay hidden. It was the inexplicable financial gains that ultimately exposed the true culprits, and that's how the CMP would build its case against Greene. Matt reached across the table and retrieved the profit and loss report that had been generated by the Joint Task Force's forensic accounting team.

Human trafficking could be broken down into three stages—recruitment/abduction, transportation, and exploitation, all of which require the exchange of money. The smart ones, like Greene, kept their financial transactions small and in line with legitimate business practices, but when examined closely, a pattern began to emerge that pointed to Greene as the leading financier and beneficiary of this particular trafficking operation. Multiple wire transfers were coming from his accounts. All were below the three thousand dollar reporting limit and from different locations. The CMP had also uncovered unusual currency deposits from overseas to U.S. accounts, which they could connect to more wire transfers to places like Richmond and Baltimore, where the Dead Rebels had established their transportation networks. But the most noticeable red flag was the use of front companies to establish accounts in the Hawala, an underground banking system based on trust, or more accurately, fear, which allowed for the transfer of payments without physically moving money through the traditional channels, eliminating the possibility of a paper trail. Greene was good, but he'd messed up when he sent a man like JC Wilks to Pikesville to get rid of Case. JC was overconfident. He'd rushed into action without fully knowing who he was up against. Now Tanner was exposed.

Matt sat the papers back on the conference table and

slumped into his high-backed chair. He'd been up for over twenty-four hours and knew he needed to sleep. Just as he'd talked himself into going home and getting some much-needed rest, his phone rang. It was Case.

"Case, what's up, buddy?"

"Not much, just squaring away a few last-minute details here at home, then I'll be headed your way. How's the target package coming along?"

"Good. We already have two observation teams outside Tanner's estate in the Catskills. One is on a company boat anchored across the Hudson. The other is on the high ground behind the property. Tanner hasn't shown up yet, but we've just confirmed he left the city with a small security contingent and a few staffers."

"And we're certain that's where he's headed?"

"His pattern of life confirmed that he seldom leaves Manhattan. He's either at his offices or his penthouse in most cases, but when he does leave, it's always to the same place."

"Good. And we're sure there's no way he can skip country?"

"No way. We've already flagged his passports with CBP and Border Patrol. Plus, we have his identifying information in the biometrics and facial recognition systems. If he goes anywhere near the border or an airport, we'll know it."

"Okay. Sounds good. I'm gonna finish up a few things here and get on the road in a couple days. I'll be there before Monday."

"No rush, brother. We have this guy on lock. We'll let him get settled into the house and give him time to feel safe. Our guys will be reporting back on any movement. Once you get here, I'll introduce you to the team, we'll pack up, head north, and hit this guy hard."

Case was quiet for a moment. "I appreciate this, Matt. I owe ya one."

"You keep saying that, and I'm gonna cash in. You know that, right?"

"I know. I'll be here when ya need me."

"Okay, my man. Hug that girl of yours for me, and drive safe. We'll see ya in a few days."

Matt hung up and leaned back in his chair just as his old FAM teammate, Ross, walked into the room.

"Ah, man." Ross moaned, pointing at the stacks of papers lying across the desk. "Please don't tell me I missed all the admin shit. You know I love the admin shit."

"Don't worry, buddy," Matt said as he stood and stretched. "I'll let you do all the after-action reports." He slapped Ross on the back, "In the meantime, I'm going home and going to bed. Tell the boss we're all set to go once Case gets here."

Ross stood there with his mouth open. "Okay. I'll let him know…but you do realize I was joking about the admin shit, right?" He yelled down the hall as Matt walked away, throwing his hand up without looking back.

"I hate admin shit, man! It was just a joke."

Chapter 6

Soft Indy rock played through the hidden speakers outside the Chi-Town coffee house where Maria Estrada stood idly wiping down the already spotless outdoor serving tables. She'd worked at the café for almost five years now, ever since she'd retired as a rehabilitation specialist, helping people with social issues find employment and independence. It wasn't that she needed the work. Her pension was enough to cover her living expenses, but she liked the atmosphere and the people who frequented the place. Most were older, around her age, late-fifties, with plenty of time on their hands. The place was seldom packed but maintained a steady flow of customers throughout the day. Maria looked up to see one of her favorites crossing the street from his house, now.

The man was fit and handsome. His gray eyes and square face were set in a gruff, emotionless expression, but shifted quickly into a warm and pleasant smile when he saw Maria looking at him.

"Good morning, Maria."

His face was freshly shaven, and he was wearing the forest green button-up shirt she liked so much.

"Good morning, August," Maria said.

August found her soft Spanish accent intoxicating.

"Are you here for your usual?"

"Sure."

"Come on inside, and I'll get it started for you," Maria tossed the towel she'd been using to clean tables over her shoulder. "Medium dark roast with two espresso shots, no room for cream, right?"

"You got it."

August held the door open so Maria could walk inside.

"How's your mother doing?" He inquired.

"Good. Thank you for asking. She's about to turn eighty-three soon, but still very active. I can barely keep up with her sometimes."

"I think it's good that you moved her in with you," August said as he sat at the small table nearest the counter. "She's lucky to have you."

Maria smiled and started August's coffee, "You want this one to go?" She asked over her shoulder.

"No. I think I'll have it here today if that's okay."

Maria brushed a lock of jet-black hair from her face and tucked it behind her ear, smiling.

"In that case, maybe I'll join you," she said, reaching for another cup. "Would that be okay with you?"

August grinned. "Yeah. That would be nice."

Maria put the two coffees on the table and sat across from August. They relaxed in comfortable silence until August finally gathered his nerve.

"Maria, could I possibly bother you for a favor?" he asked, looking down into his mug.

"Sure."

"I have to go out of town on business for a couple weeks. I usually keep DJ, my cat, at the kennel, but it's—"

"I'd be happy to watch your cat for you, August," Maria interrupted.

The man didn't know how to respond. He'd obviously rehearsed how to phrase the question, and the immediate reply threw him off.

"I'd pay you, of course. If that's—"

Maria cut him off again. "August, you've been coming here and talking with me almost every morning for four years. It's about time you asked me for something other than coffee." She said, hoping the man would take the hint. He did.

August nodded. "Okay then, how about when I get back, I take you to dinner? Just the two of us. As a way of saying thank you."

Maria's brilliant smile flashed from across the table, but she said nothing.

"What?" August asked, thinking that he'd somehow blown his shot.

"Nothing's wrong. I'd love to go to dinner with you. It just took you long enough to ask."

"Well, some things have changed lately, and I'm going to have a little more free time when I get back—time I'd like to spend with you. If you wouldn't mind."

Maria sipped at her mug. Her dark hazel eyes locked onto August. "I'd like that a lot."

August walked back across 110th Street feeling good about how things had gone with Maria. He'd wanted to ask her out for a very long time, but there was no way he would have introduced her into his life before retiring. Once this job was finished, he could finally start over, build the average, everyday life he craved and be free of all the corrupt assholes who paid him to do the things they were too cowardly to do themselves. The thought was so appealing that it pulled his mind away from the job, but he caught himself.

"Fuck!" He grumbled, "Stop thinking like a love-sick teenager and focus up. You've still got work to do."

Chapter 7

The Village of Athens, New York, sat perched in the Catskill Mountains against the western bank of the Hudson River directly across from the island of Middle Ground Flats. Settled in the late 17th century, the town's close proximity to the river and its tributaries made it a thriving hub for shipbuilders, brick-makers, and ice harvesters. Now, Athens housed an eclectic group of artisans, entrepreneurs, and families who preferred the quiet charm of village living to the pandemonium of life in a big city, so when four black SUVs turned off Route 385 and snaked their way toward Water Street and the estate of Tanner Greene, everyone turned to stare.

Once the convoy reached the end of Water Street, they turned into the gated, tree-lined driveway that led to the sprawling estate. The house was massive. Its three stories of stone and stucco sat on an immaculately kept fifty-one acres and dwarfed the other residences in or around Athens. Its lawns were expansive and dotted with formal gardens and groves of mature White Oaks. The backyard accommodated the pool, pool house, and tennis courts, then sloped gradually toward the river, where water lapped at the edges of the boathouse and private dock. The entire property was surrounded by an eight-foot security fence and patrolled year-round by two very big and intimidating Doberman Pinschers—Bruno and Silas.

Gravel crunched beneath the SUV's Yokohama off-road tires as the small convoy came to a halt in the circular drive.

A four-man security detail fanned out and kept watch while Tanner and his personal assistant, Celia Hudson, exited their vehicle and moved hurriedly toward the house. They had two other people with them—a young man and what looked like a teenage girl trying her best to keep up. They were met at the door by Ms. Margaret Adderley, the housekeeper, who tried not to look perplexed by the unexpected arrival of Mr. Greene.

"Good morning, sir. When I received word you were coming, I—"

"No time for any of that now, Ms. Adderley," Tanner said dismissively. "My assistant and I will settle into the master suite upstairs. I want my security detail to station themselves wherever they deem appropriate. These two," Tanner said, indicating the man and very young-looking woman, "are employees of mine and can sleep downstairs. I'll only discuss the particulars of my stay with the members of my security team. What I need from you and your staff are clean sheets, cooked meals, and to stay the hell out of my way, understood?"

Ms. Adderley bristled at the tone Greene took with her but knew better than to protest. "Yes, sir. We'll get your things situated and be at your service should you need anything else."

Greene walked past the woman without acknowledgment and into the house.

Celia and the other woman looked apologetically at Ms. Adderley as they sheepishly followed, too afraid to speak.

Margaret looked out toward the heavily armed security detail in the driveway and back at Tanner, who strode up the wide spiraled staircase leading to the upper rooms. She turned back to see Walter, the groundskeeper, standing beside the portico stairs, wiping his big, dirt-covered hands with an equally dirty handkerchief. He wore his standard blue pinstriped coveralls and turned his weather-beaten face toward Ms. Adderley with a pleasant smile.

"I see the boss is back in town. Any idea what this is about?" He asked.

Margaret's usually cheerful face appeared tight and troubled. "I have no idea, Walter. But whatever business he has here, I hope it's over soon."

Since the death of Mike Moretti, Sanji Reed had taken over as the head of Mr. Greene's security detail. His dark eyes scanned the vast estate while he waited patiently for Tanner and his entourage to enter the house. Once he saw everyone safely inside, he began barking orders at the other three men.

"Monroe, Flores, grab the bags and start moving everything inside. Collins post up outside Mr. Greene's quarters and radio back to me once he's settled. I'll gather up the house staff."

The three men nodded curtly and rushed to their assignments. Sanji walked across the crushed marble drive toward the nervously awaiting Ms. Adderley and her imposing companion.

He made no introduction. "Mr. Greene will be staying here at the estate for an undetermined period. Send all of your staff away except for those absolutely necessary for the upkeep of the property and running of the household. Two groundskeepers and five housemaids should be sufficient. That's to include yourself. Everyone else needs to go. While Mr. Greene is on the grounds, there will be no cellphones or other communication devices that aren't tied directly to Mr. Greene's private server. If anyone is caught with one, they'll be fired on the spot. Got it?"

The man and woman nodded without speaking.

"Good. Now, go pick the staff who'll be staying. Tell them

what I just told you and report back to the house immediately. Ms. Hudson will have nondisclosure agreements for everyone to sign. After that, you can go about your business."

The pair looked at each other, confused.

"Go," Sanji said, leaning forward, "We don't have time to waste."

The man and woman hurried away in different directions. Sanji tried to hide it, but in truth, even he didn't know why they'd been rushed out of the city or why he was forced to sign yet another NDA. Greene didn't make a habit of explaining himself to the "help," but despite his silence on the matter, this trip felt more secretive and urgent than most, which was concerning for Sanji—especially since it was only his first week as Greene's chief security officer.

Chapter 8

Tinted light spilled through the massive floor-to-ceiling windows that lined the main concourse of Charlotte Douglas International Airport. August Moody walked calmly through the bustling crowd on his way to the exit, perfectly aware that he was being followed. The man tailing him hadn't been on his flight but had dropped in behind him near the food court, staying just close enough that he wouldn't be seen, or so he thought.

The man was skinny but not in a sickly way, more like a long-distance runner. His blond hair was oiled and pushed straight back on top of his head, above a face adorned with several piercings and two small tattoos—a little diamond below his right eye and one above his left eyebrow that read, *repent*. August walked slowly past the rows of white rocking chairs lining the atrium, then sped up. The man following him looked around casually and continued without altering his pace. He was good.

August decided to test the man further, so he stopped short of the baggage claim exit and turned. The skinny man didn't miss a beat. He didn't pause or change directions. He knew his target would have to come through baggage claim eventually, so he looked past August without making eye contact and continued through the exit door as if he were any other passenger—impressive. August waited a few seconds longer, giving his tail time to situate himself on the other side, then followed him out. After a quick scan of the area, the man seemed to have vanished entirely.

On alert, August wove through the crowd of passengers collecting their luggage and reuniting with loved ones. He walked outside, carrying his leather duffle, into the cacophony of car horns and traffic whistles, then across the pedestrian walkway to the rent-a-car building, keeping his eyes peeled for further surveillance. Once inside, August presented his ID and reservation confirmation to the man behind the Enterprise counter and waited patiently.

After a long and tedious line of questioning about supplemental car insurance, the process was over. "Here you are, sir. A beige four-door sedan, just like you requested," the man said enthusiastically, dropping the keys into August's outstretched hand. "You'll find it in slot B13. Have a safe trip, Mr. White."

August curled his mouth into a forced smile and proceeded through the automated doors to the parking area. He looked left and right until he found row B marked on one of the immense support pillars, then walked down the aisle, counting spaces in his head until he reached slot number 13. The man who'd been following him stood there, arms crossed and smiling. One silver tooth gleaming in the light above his head.

"You couldn't have rented something sexier than a Buick?" He asked.

"Beige Buicks don't draw attention, kid."

"Cheapskate."

August shook his head and grinned, "Hello, Joe. It's good to see ya again."

The two men shook hands and hugged, slapping each other on the back. "It's good to see you too, Augie…or…I'm sorry. It's Mr. White now, isn't it?"

August smirked and unlocked the car door. "You know how much I love Reservoir Dogs, Joe. Now shut up and get in."

August turned off the 85 onto I-77 North toward Pikesville, Virginia. Joe sat in the passenger seat, studying the target package August had received from Senator Whitlock.

"Jesus, Augie. I don't like this at all. This guy isn't like the other jobs."

"I know," August said, nodding his head. "That's why the pay is double and why I called on you to help."

Joe flipped through the folder and started rattling off facts that August already knew.

"Army Ranger, purple heart, fucking two bronze stars, and, oh…as a civilian—the Secretary of Defense medal of bravery for actions in the face of grave danger. Fuck, man. This isn't just some corporate whistleblower, Augie. This guy's like fucking Rambo. Why would anybody want him dead?"

August turned to Joe without acknowledging his very valid concerns, "You know that foul mouth of yours is one of the reasons nobody likes you, right?"

Joe flashed his silver tooth in a wide grin, "Really? I assumed they were all just jealous of my good looks."

August scoffed, "Anyway. Any overt action against this guy is gonna draw a lot of attention, so it's important this one goes down looking like an accident—just some random tragic thing that took a good man's life way too soon."

"You got a plan?" Joe asked.

"Not yet, but I have some ideas. We've got about another hour on the road." August said, glancing at his watch, "I booked us a room at some roadside motel on this side of the Virginia border. It's about twenty minutes from Pikesville. I'd rather limit our exposure on target, so we'll keep a safe distance."

"Why?"

August kept both hands on the wheel and nodded toward

the file, "Keep reading. There's a rundown of what happened there just a little over a week ago. A man was sent down from Richmond to get rid of Younger, and the whole thing went sideways. Now, Younger and everyone around him will be on high alert. We have to be careful."

"Understood."

Joe dove back into the file, and August focused on the road as he thought back to his time in the Marine Corps and his first encounter with Joe.

August was serving as a Drill Instructor at Paris Island when he met the seventeen-year-old Marine recruit. Joe had come up from Florida, a poor kid from a broken home who wore his abuse like the tattoos he would eventually embrace. Still, August saw promise in him. He was intelligent, quick to pick up new skills, and clearly committed to becoming a good Marine. August took a particular interest in Joe's career, and after he'd served the appropriate amount of time in a conventional unit, August referred Joe to the three-week MARSOC assessment and selection course. Joe passed with flying colors. After that, he went on to the grueling nine-month Individual Training Course at the Marine Special Operations School in Camp Lejeune, North Carolina. From there, August lost track of Joe, but their paths crossed again in Iraq and Afghanistan. As the Global War on Terror, or the GWOT, as it was known in military terms, began to wind down, Joe started getting into trouble. Like too many other Marines who had survived wartime deployments, he found it difficult to readjust to life outside of combat. His commanding officers, in deference to his outstanding service, "asked" Joe to forgo reenlistment or else be removed from the Corps for disciplinary issues. After running out the remainder of his enlistment, Joe left the Corps and returned to Florida, where he tried fitting back into civilian life, but that didn't work. Joe eventually fell in with the wrong crowd, stealing and selling oxy outside Tampa. At this point, August had retired and moved into the private sector, doing what he did best—killing. He had reached out and offered Joe some work, with the understanding that he would clean himself up and stay under the radar with the police. Joe quickly latched onto the lifeline his old Drill Instructor had tossed him. This was the only life he'd ever understood.

Joe finished reading just as August pulled off the interstate and onto a broad two-lane highway that, if followed north, would lead directly into downtown Pikesville. August glanced over at Joe, who rubbed his eyes and stared out the windshield.

"You good?"

Joe slammed the folder shut and looked back at August with eyes so dark they were hard to read. Most of the jobs he'd helped Augie with were easier for him to justify—vindictive employees using company secrets to extort money from the people who fired them, corporate rivals, and traitors. Things were always easier if he could find a way to rationalize the work he did, but this time, the target was the kind of man Joe looked up to.

August stared doggedly at Joe, "Well?"

Joe shook his head, "Semper Fi, Augie. Let's just get this done."

Chapter 9

Sam walked into the bedroom just as Case dragged his deployment bag from the closet and tossed it on the floor beside the bed. He stood there, looking around the room with his hands on his hips, deciding where he should start.

"You packing already?" She asked as she shut the door quietly behind her. "I thought we still had a couple of days."

"We do," Case answered. "I just wanted to get a few things organized. I have a lot more to pack now that Matt and Ross left all this gear."

Sam watched without saying anything, but Case could tell that she was troubled by the look on her face.

"Hey, are you okay?" He asked.

"It just makes me nervous, is all."

Case looked around at the assorted weapons, radios, and bits of tactical equipment strewn about the room. Sam crossed her arms, afraid to say more lest she start crying. She wanted to be strong so Case could focus on his mission without distraction. Case stopped what he was doing and walked around the bed to Sam, putting his hand beneath her chin and lifting her face until she looked him in the eyes.

"Sam, you said it yourself. This needs to end. And as soon as we take down Greene, I'm turning all this crap in and coming straight back home to you, okay?"

Sam grabbed Case's hand and held it, "I believe you, Case. I understand why it's all happening, but I need to know that it ends with this. This all has to stop if there's ever gonna be a chance for us. I need you to finish this, then let it go. You know that, right?"

Case took a deep breath and let it out. He knew that he sometimes needed the danger and chaos to feel whole. But it was something he was willing to leave behind if it meant hanging on to the person he loved most.

"I promise, Sam. Once this is done, I'm home forever."

"Okay, I'm holding you to that," Sam said as she pushed away from Case and started getting ready for bed.

Case looked around the room and decided packing could wait. He put his Daniel Defense Short-Barrel rifle, Glock 19, spare magazines, and ammo away in the safe, kicked everything else into a corner, then sat on the edge of the bed and unlaced his well-worn Silverado work boots.

"How's Mia? Is she sleeping any better?" Case asked as he pried the boots from his feet and set them next to the bed.

Sam stood in front of the dresser mirror and looked at Case in the reflection as she removed her earrings—two tiny gold studs Case had once given her for Valentine's Day when they were still in high school.

"She's sleeping a little better now. I think she just tried to bury everything instead of coping with it, and it's finally caught up with her."

"And you?" Case asked. "Are you gonna be alright?"

Sam's face hardened in the mirror. "I'm okay Case. That doesn't mean I don't worry. And whether you're here or not, I'll never let anything like that happen again."

Case's eyes drifted into the distance. Sam knew he felt responsible for what had happened the night Mia was taken and needed him to understand that, despite the trauma they'd experienced, a lot of good had come from the incident as well.

"You know that girl you found up north, Tammy Lynn?"

Before burning the Dead Rebels bar down in Richmond, Case had rescued several girls who were being held by the club. One of them, Tammy Lynn, had been taken from Pikesville as she walked home from school. She was only fourteen at the time.

"Her and Mia have been hanging out a lot lately. I think it helps both of them to have someone to talk to."

"That's good," Case said flatly.

Sam could see Case was beating himself up over how things had turned out and walked over to sit down beside him.

"None of those young women would be here today if it weren't for you, Case. You may feel responsible for what happened to me and Mia, but Tammy Lynn and the other girls, well, now they're at home, safe in their own beds because of what you did."

Case looked at Sam and forced a smile to his lips before leaning over and kissing her on the cheek. He understood what Sam was doing, and he appreciated it.

"I don't know what I'd do without you, Sam."

Sam put her arm around Case's shoulder and let out an exaggerated sigh. "To be honest, neither do I."

Chapter 10
Pikesville, Virginia
1992

Eleven-year-old Tina Scott had never known who her father was. But then again, there was a lot Tina didn't know. She didn't know that she was really born in Richmond or that she had a twin brother. Tina also didn't know why she had such a hard time controlling her impulses, which was how she'd ended up punching Nancy Fodrell in the face for calling her poor.

Ms. Akers, the sixth-grade English teacher, broke the girls up and marched them down to Principal Goodwin's office. The man met the trio at the door with his arms folded. Nancy was the first to go inside, while Tina waited on the bench in the hallway with Ms. Akers.

Diane Akers had taught elementary school for a long time and had dealt with all types of children, but Tina Scott was a different kind of challenge. Although her father wasn't present at home, her mother, Vera, seemed happy and stable. They didn't have much in terms of wealth, but most of the kids in her class came from low-income families. Some were just poorer than others. Diane decided to do a little probing.

"Tina. I have to ask. Is everything okay at home?"

"Yes. Ma'am, why?"

"I just can't seem to figure you out, is all. Your mother keeps to herself but seems like a nice person, and it appears that you two have a good relationship. You're smart and you know you're no poorer than Nancy in there. So, for the life of me, I can't figure out why you lose your cool the way you do, or where that part of you comes from."

Tina thought about it briefly, "My daddy, maybe."

"Was he an impulsive man?"

"Impulsive?" Tina asked, confused by the word.

"Did he do things he didn't always know how to explain?"

Tina shrugged, "I never met my daddy. But Mom tells me I'm a lot like him sometimes. She says that when she's mad at me."

"And is that very often? Her being mad at you?"

"No. Only when I do things like this."

"Well, you and I are going to work on this impulsive behavior of yours, okay? You're a good girl, Tina, and I don't like you getting into all this trouble, so when Mr. Goodwin calls you in. I want you to apologize to Nancy and admit you overreacted to her name-calling. If you can do that, I'll put in a good word with the principal, and we'll try to keep you out of detention and out of trouble with your mom. Does that sound fair to you?"

Tina nodded, "Okay. I'll apologize to Nancy. Thanks, Ms. Akers."

Diane patted Tina on the knee and waited with her until Mr. Goodwin stepped into the hall.

As he held the door open and Tina ambled inside, Ms. Akers couldn't help but feel bad for the girl. She'd worked with enough kids from broken homes to see how the absence of a parent affected them. Sometimes, in cases of abuse, the absence was necessary for the safety of the child, but kids seldom saw it that way. They always tended to blame themselves. Diane hoped that one day Tina would find a good man of her own, build upon the life her mother had provided, and create something new for her own children. That's not always how things worked out, but Diane had high hopes for Tina. The girl just needed someone to show her how valuable she really was.

Chapter 11
Present Day

Once August hit the town of Mount Airy, North Carolina, he pulled off the Andy Griffith Parkway into the immaculately kept parking lot of the Mayberry Motor Inn. The place was submerged in a sea of green. Massive white oaks and silver maples filled the courtyard, surrounding the communal pavilion. A small rectangular pool shimmered in the front, encircled by a white picket fence and neat rows of small plastic tables flanked by matching vinyl chairs. The motel's most notable feature was the vintage black and white 1962 Ford Galaxy squad car parked by the main entrance. A relic from the television show that the town had inspired.

"What the fuck, Augie. This town doesn't have a Marriott?"

August shook his head. "You have no appreciation for history, Joe. This place is pure Americana. It's the town Mayberry's based on."

Joe stared blankly at August.

"Mayberry, *The Andy Griffith Show*—Andy and Opie, Barney Fife, none of that rings a bell?"

Joe knew full well what August was talking about, but liked to push the old man's buttons once in a while. "Never heard of it."

August grunted and looked out the window.

The building itself was built in 1967. It was a charming, single-story red brick structure with spotless white trim and twenty-seven rooms numbered left to right. The main lobby was situated in the center.

August threw the Buick into park and opened the driver's side door. "Wait here. I doubt whoever's working the counter's ever seen a man as ugly as you. We don't need them asking any questions."

Joe rolled his eyes and did as he was told, but not without an audible "Smartass" as Moody slammed the door.

Once inside the small, wood-paneled lobby, August was met by an elderly lady who smiled pleasantly and greeted him with a "Hey there, mister, and welcome to Mayberry."

August didn't know if the woman was serious or if this was all just part of some touristy shtick, so he kept his tone professional.

"Hello, ma'am. I called ahead. The name's White. I booked a room for three nights."

There was no laptop or computer terminal behind the counter. The woman simply swiveled in her chair to retrieve a set of keys from a small brass hook.

"You'll be in room 17, sir. That'll be two hundred and sixty-one dollars for the three nights. But if you have an AARP card, we can knock that down to an even two hundred for ya."

August grimaced at the comment. He hated being treated like a senior citizen. "I'm sorry, I don't have an AARP membership, and my credit cards were recently stolen. I'm still waiting on the replacements. I believe you take cash, though, correct?"

The woman frowned sympathetically, "Oh, sweetheart, I'm so sorry to hear that. Of course, we still take cash. I'll just need you to sign the ledger right here," she said as she placed the sizeable yellow book on the counter in front of her and indicated a blank space at the bottom of the page.

August scribbled *Mr. A. White* in the book, opened his wallet, and handed the lady three one-hundred-dollar bills.

She didn't mark them with a counterfeit bill detector or hold them to the light to check for watermarks. She simply opened the cash register, placed the bills in the appropriate slot, and counted out August's change. People in this part of the country were generally friendly and overly trusting, which made August's job much easier.

After accepting his change and thanking the woman behind the counter, August returned to the car and got inside.

"We going to the room? Joe asked. "I could use a shower."

"You're telling me," August smirked as he started the Buick and backed out of the parking spot. "But we need to go do some shopping first."

Chapter 12

The master suite of Greene's estate home was enormous, with a large stone fireplace along the eastern wall, a well-appointed sitting room, and a walk-in closet that dwarfed Celia's tiny New York apartment. It would have been the perfect spot for a dream vacation had it not been for the company she was forced to keep. Celia didn't want to be here. She'd been blackmailed into working for Tanner before graduating college—a victim of coercion after being drugged and raped by a person she thought she could trust. Now, her whole life was spent in the servitude of a man who got off on hurting the people around him. A man whose money and influence gave him control over the one thing he hated most—women. On top of his already repulsive nature, Tanner had never been one to handle stress very well. Since leaving the city, Celia knew it would only be a matter of time before he took his frustrations, whatever they may be, out on her.

Celia finished unpacking her things and looked through the large French doors that led out to the covered balcony. The Hudson River flowed slowly in the background, unencumbered by the lives of the people it sustained. The waterway was named after Henry Hudson, an English explorer who sailed up the river in 1609 while working for the Dutch East India Company. Celia wondered if they might be related. In the distance, Tanner Greene strode along the edge of the swimming pool, speaking angrily into his phone. She'd never seen him this way—scared—but his fear brought her a deep sense of comfort and satisfaction. As she watched him, she imagined Tanner falling into the pool and drowning. No, not drowning—that would be too easy. It needed to be something more dramatic and violent.

Celia jumped when the housekeeper, Ms. Adderley, spoke up from the doorway.

"Hello, Ms. Hudson. I have the staff gathered downstairs. I understand there's something for them to sign."

"Oh, yes, of course," Celia said as she regained her composure. "I'll get everything together and meet you in the main foyer."

Margaret could see that the woman was agitated. She'd met Celia several times before, and there had always been an undercurrent of stress about her. She knew Mr. Greene could be difficult to work for, but this seemed different. The tension was palpable.

"Ma'am, I don't mean to pry, but is everything okay?"

Celia could see the concern in Ms. Adderley's eyes, but didn't know what to say, so she deflected. "It'll all be fine. Let's just get these forms signed and filed so everyone can go about their business."

"Yes, ma'am," Margaret started, "About the forms. The staff are a bit concerned, what with the added security and sending the other employees home. Is there anything we should know about?"

Celia couldn't bring herself to lie to the woman. But she couldn't risk telling her everything she knew. That would only cause more problems.

"Margaret, I want you to do me a favor, okay?"

Margaret nodded. "Of course, Ms. Hudson. Whatever you need."

Celia stepped past the older woman and looked down the hallway to ensure none of Tanner's security team was listening. "Margaret, once these nondisclosure agreements are signed, I want you and your staff to stay as far away from the main house as possible. Do whatever you have to do to keep up appearances, but limit your exposure to Mr. Greene if you can. Do you understand?"

"Yes, ma'am, I do," Ms. Adderley said, straightening her back a bit. She'd never had children of her own, so she'd always been overly protective of the young women who worked for her. She had to ask. "Ma'am, are we in any danger?"

Celia looked crestfallen. "I certainly hope not, Margaret. But if that changes, you'll be the first person to know, I promise."

Satisfied with the answer, Ms. Adderley turned and left the room. Celia returned to the small desk by the double doors and gathered the NDA forms. Tanner was no longer on the phone but continued pacing along the pool's edge with his hands clasped behind his back. She knew things were going to get bad here at some point. The question now was when it would happen and how she could best protect the good people who worked for such a horrible man.

Chapter 13

It was getting close to noon the next day when Joe walked out to the pool carrying his cell phone and a blue plastic Walmart bag. The sun was bright and high, but the temperature was tolerable, unlike the sweltering Florida heat he'd grown up in. He wore a pair of tattered knee-length cargo shorts, unlaced work boots, and an unbuttoned floral shirt that revealed several randomly placed tattoos, the largest of which sat in the center of his chest. It was a big square standing on its point with a skull and crossbones in the center. The word *TOXIC* was inked below it in large, jagged letters. A woman sat close to the pool's edge, watching her two young sons splash in the shallow end when Joe walked in. He smiled politely and closed the gate behind him, but the woman failed to smile back. He knew what would happen next.

As if on cue, the woman shouted calmly across the water, "Boys, grab your things. It's time for us to go."

The splashing stopped abruptly, and the boys looked at each other. "But Mom! We just got here," the oldest boy yelled back.

"Yeah, Mom. Just a little longer, pleeeease." Pleaded the youngest.

"Boys, your father is waiting in the room and—"

"But dad's not even—"

"Now, Steven! Out of the pool!"

The two boys saw the furious look in their mother's eyes and did as they were told without any further objections.

Joe didn't take offense to the situation. He knew what he

looked like. It was an image he'd cultivated over time, and it served a very valuable purpose. It kept people at a distance, and that's exactly what he needed now—some space.

"You heard your mother, kids, get the fuck out," Joe said as he dropped his bag on an empty table by the end of the pool.

Appalled, the woman stood and strode to the shallow end, her bare feet smacking against the wet concrete. She helped the boys out of the water, wrapped them in their towels, and ushered them toward the exit. Joe waved as the woman slammed the gate closed behind her.

"You folks enjoy your stay here in Mayberry." He yelled behind them as they rushed across the parking lot to the safety of their room. "Or whatever the fuck this place is called," he mumbled to himself. Once alone, Joe sat down, opened the Walmart bag, and removed the Apple Air Tag Augie had purchased the night before.

It didn't take long to set up. Joe could now use his phone to track the tag's location from anywhere. That was step one. Step two would be to place the tag on Case Younger's vehicle so he and Augie could keep an eye on his location without getting too close. It was a smart move, given the man's training and experience.

Joe heard the gate open again and saw August walking toward the pool with two motel coffees and a folded newspaper.

"How's it going?" The older man asked.

"Good. I have everything set up and ready to go. What's next?"

August put the coffees on the table, sat next to Joe, and opened his copy of the Mount Airy News. "We know Younger is going after this guy, Tanner Greene, that means he'll be leaving Pikesville at some point, but we don't know when. We have to move quick. You'll plant the tracker tonight, and we'll try to gather as much information as possible about Younger's movements. Then we'll figure out the best way to make the hit. Once he leaves, it's safe to assume he'll be making a pitstop in McLean to recruit help from his friends. Things'll get exponentially more complicated from there, so it'll be best to hit him sooner rather than later."

"His friends in McLean—are those the same guys who helped him out with the Wilks fiasco?"

August nodded and sipped his coffee, "Like I said, it's best if he never makes it that far north."

Joe considered the situation. He had misgivings about the assignment and decided it would be best to voice his concerns. "Hittin' this dude isn't going to be easy, Augie. Even if we pull it off, there's no guarantee it'll fully protect Whitlock or this guy Greene. It seems to me like killing Younger is just putting band-aids on a bullet wound, and it's exposing us to a whole lot of risk."

August removed his reading glasses and set his newspaper aside. "Joe, I understand you're a little uneasy about this job, but guys like us can't concern ourselves with the bigger picture. We get the job, we do the job, we get paid. That's it. Right now, killing Case Younger is the job, and that job came from Senator Whitlock, not Tanner Greene. Whatever Greene is up to is none of our concern."

Joe nodded, "Understood. When do we leave?"

August slid a piece of paper across the small table to Joe, "You're on your own tonight, pal. I need to call a friend of mine to check on my cat. Here's the address and a description of the truck."

Joe read the paper and shoved it into his shirt pocket.

"It looks like the place is in the middle of nowhere." August continued, "Just wait till dark, keep the car out of sight, get in, get out—that's it."

"I can do that."

"Good. This is your job now, Joe. I'm just here to make sure it all goes smooth. You good with that?"

Joe sat up and nodded. August had never been the type of man to put much faith in other people. Joe took the responsibility he was being given seriously. "Hoorah, Augie. I won't let you down."

Chapter 14

It had been a long day on the farm, but Case enjoyed the effort it took to keep everything running smoothly. He liked keeping the fields clear and the fences patched. He loved working on the old red and white International tractor his dad had taught him to operate when he was just a boy, and feeding the cattle. It was the life he'd always longed for—simple and complete.

The sun had just started slipping toward the western ridge as Case plopped himself into one of the porch rocking chairs and looked over the green fields, satisfied with the day's work. Sam and Mia walked outside and joined Case in the fresh air as they did most evenings. Sam practically fell into the rocker beside Case while Mia sat on the far side of the steps with her back against the railing, texting Trevor. Before tackling the fieldwork, Case had spent most of the morning packing his gear and making last-minute preparations for his trip to McLean. All he needed to do now was load the truck and go, but that was always the hardest part. Sam had spent the day busying herself with mundane tasks around the house to take her mind off the fact that Case was leaving again.

"Do you know what time you'll be hittin' the road?" Sam asked.

"I'm in no rush. I'll probably head out the day after tomorrow. If I leave early on Sunday, I'll be less likely to hit that beltway traffic up north."

"You're not worried about this guy, Greene, slipping away?"

Case shook his head, "Not at all. The CMP has eyes all over him. We want him to get settled and start feeling safe—let his guard down a little before we hit him. Plus, he'll want to start covering his bases and reaching out to the people in his network, which could expose more links in the trafficking chain."

Sam knew Case was a strategic thinker and that any plans he had made with Matt and Ross would be well thought out. Affirming these little details was just her way of letting the man she loved know she was worried about him.

She didn't want Case to start overthinking things, so she shifted to another topic. "Maybe before you load everything up tomorrow, you can take me and Mia to the diner for breakfast."

Case sat up a little straighter, "That sounds good. Then maybe you and I can spend a little quality time together before I go."

Sam grinned seductively, "Quality time sounds nice."

"Jeez! Will you two cut it out already." Mia said as she stood from her perch on the stairs. "You're worse than a couple of school kids, for goodness' sake."

Mia had been so quiet that Case had forgotten she was there. His face reddened with embarrassment, and he quickly shifted to a different subject. "Since we're on the topic of school kids, what's Trevor been up to lately? I haven't seen him much in the past couple of days. Is he doin' okay?"

Mia knew why Trevor had been keeping his distance from Case, but promised she wouldn't mention it in front of the adults.

"Yeah, he's doin' great. Just busy with school stuff. I was actually going to walk over to see him now if that's okay."

"Sure, sweetie," Sam said from her rocker. "Tell him and Dimpsey we said hello and invite them over for supper tomorrow night. It'd be nice for us to all sit down and have a meal together before Case leaves."

"Okay," Mia said as she stepped off the porch and started down the long driveway. "I'll be gone for about an hour. Just in case you two need some *quality time*."

"Jesus," Case whispered under his breath, shaking his head, regretting that he'd ever made the comment.

Sam looked at him seriously, "What? You wouldn't like some quality time?"

Case sat quietly, rocking back and forth as Mia hit the end of the driveway and crossed the road toward Dimpsey's. Once she was out of sight, he hoisted himself from his chair and sauntered toward the screen door without saying a word. Sam stayed put, trying her best to look indifferent as she gazed across the open field in front of the house. She heard the slow creak of rusty old hinges and waited. A loving smile came to her lips when Case finally spoke.

"You coming?"

It was almost midnight when the house finally went dark. Joe had parked the Buick on a short rise above the farm where he could keep an eye on the place without being seen. The lights were on in the house when he got there, and he hadn't been parked long when he saw a young woman walk up the long driveway from across the street. She went inside, closed the front door behind her, and shut the porch light off but stayed awake for another hour before finally turning in. After the last lights went out, Joe gave it another hour, then went to work.

He had disabled the interior lights of the Buick so they

wouldn't illuminate when he opened the door. Joe slipped out quietly and climbed through the barbed wire fence to his right. That put him in the field behind the farm with plenty of cover between him and the house. From his position on the rise, he saw that Case's truck had been parked inside the barn. *Good.* That would lessen his chances of being seen or heard as he planted the tracker.

Joe had been meticulous in his planning. He'd disassembled the Air Tag and removed its tiny internal speaker to keep the device from alerting anyone to its presence. He'd also purchased a strong magnetic box that could house the tracker and make it easier to secure. Once he reached the barn, Joe took a minute to assess his surroundings. Everything was calm and quiet, so he retrieved the small red-lensed penlight from his pocket and looked around. The big Dodge Power Wagon sat in the center of the barn, surrounded by hay bales and old pieces of rusty farm equipment. Joe didn't want to risk opening the door or disturbing the vehicle in any way, so he quickly placed the tracker in its magnetic box and secured it to the truck's steel frame behind the transmission mount. After that, Joe looked around the vehicle to ensure he hadn't left any debris or footprints, then checked the G-Shock Mudmaster on his wrist. He'd been on target for less than seven minutes. Satisfied with his work, Joe quickly made his way back to the Buick, took out his cell phone, and made sure the tracker was pinging its location. *Gotcha.* Joe then shot a quick text to August.

"All set. Headed back now."

Joe threw the car into drive and pulled away slowly. It would be a thirty-minute drive back to the motel, then he could finally get some much-needed sleep. He needed to be well-rested for tomorrow.

Chapter 15

Tanner was growing impatient. He'd been on hold for nearly twenty minutes waiting for Senator Whitlock to pick up the phone. Finally, just as he was hitting the peak of his frustration, a flat, feminine voice came across the line.

"Mr. Greene, I'm sorry, but—"

"Where the fuck is Glen, Evelin. He's not returning my calls?"

The woman on the other end cleared her throat but maintained an even and professional tone. "Sir, I'm the Senator's legislative director, not his secretary. He'll be tied up in meetings most of the morning and won't be able to speak with you today. I suggest you schedule future calls through his personal assistant, the same way everyone else does."

Tanner had dealt with Evelin before and always disliked the woman's assertiveness.

"Listen to me, Evelin," Tanner hissed angrily, "You tell that overinflated clown that I need to speak with him immediately and that if he intends to keep his seat in office, he will call me back at his earliest fucking convenience. I need confirmation that the help he promised is on the way. Can you remember all that, Evelin?"

The woman paused to compose herself. She'd never liked Tanner Greene, but dealing with self-important assholes like him seemed to be a big part of her job.

"I'll pass your message along to the Senator, Mr. Greene. Have a pleasant evening."

The line went dead. Tanner sat at his desk, feeling his blood come to a boil. God, the things he'd like to do to that woman. Unfortunately, those fantasies would have to wait. What Tanner didn't understand was how Whitlock could be so stupid. The man knew what was at stake. Surely, he could comprehend what ignoring a situation like this would do to his career, his future, and his family.

Tanner opened his laptop and logged into the video-sharing software his company had helped fund. Initially developed for use within the intel community, the program could also be used for more nefarious applications. Within it were several secure portals that could only be accessed by those with the appropriate alphanumeric passcode. That code was autogenerated every sixty seconds and displayed on the small RSA token Tanner kept on his keychain. Once inside, authorized users could send and receive encrypted videos through a random VPN generator, ensuring that neither the sender nor receiver could be identified.

Tanner then went to his thumb drive and opened a series of password-protected folders and subfolders until he came to one labeled "insurance." He opened it and scrolled through a grid of thumbnails until he found what he was looking for. Tanner clicked on the file labeled GW061819 and dragged it over to the video-sharing software, then dropped it into the folder only Senator Whitlock had access to. Once uploaded, he opened up his email and typed a quick message.

Glen,
Check your inbox. If I fall, you fall with me.
TG

It was a desperate measure, but necessary. Like many politicians, Whitlock had some shady connections that helped him out of sticky situations from time to time. The video Tanner had was his only assurance that those connections could be used to his benefit. Now, all he could do was wait.

The video was shot with a hidden infrared camera, giving everything in the room a glowing, ghostly appearance. There was a dresser along one wall with a television hung above it, and a king-size bed pressed against the other. The bed was flanked on either side by two nightstands. One held a reading lamp, and the other a phone and alarm clock. A closed door leading into a small bathroom was visible opposite the camera. Glen Whitlock recognized the room. He knew the hotel, and he knew what would happen next.

There was no mistaking the girl for anything other than what she was—a scared child barely old enough to drive. Whitlock watched the video in abject horror, remembering bits and pieces of what had occurred that evening. During his campaign run, he'd been visiting New York and had made time for drinks with his most prominent donor, Tanner Greene. They'd met in the bar of a hotel Greene owned, and before long, he'd gotten too drunk to attempt the trip back to DC. Tanner graciously offered him a suite and even made a few phone calls to arrange for some "company" later in the evening. Whitlock had accepted as he always did.

The girl stood by the bed in the center of the room, wearing a slim spaghetti-strap dress. Her head hung low, and she swayed back and forth as if she were about to pass out. Whitlock watched as his own image entered the frame, and he felt himself begin to sweat. In the infrared light, his eyes looked black and demonic. He stood behind the girl and touched the soft skin of her arms, kissing her neck. His hands slowly swept outward, pushing the straps from her shoulders. The dress fell to the ground, and Whitlock turned the girl to face him. He tried kissing her lips, but she turned her head defiantly. That's when he shoved her to the bed and took off his belt.

He couldn't keep watching. Whitlock slammed the laptop closed and rested his aching head in his hands. He'd known the video existed. Tanner had referred to it several times when he needed help with one of his problems, but this was the first time he'd seen it himself. It wasn't what he'd done to the girl that scared him—it was the looming existence of the video. If this leaked to the press, it would destroy everything he'd built over two decades of public service. Whitlock couldn't let some drunken indiscretion tear everything apart. Tanner Greene would have to be dealt with.

Chapter 16

August drove to a small farmers market that sat on the Virginia/North Carolina border and waited. Early morning customers strolled in and out of the open-air structure carrying armloads of colorful flowers, fresh vegetables, and locally sourced items such as honey and homemade preserves. August was considering going inside and finding something nice for Maria when the tiny blue dot on his phone started to move. August downed the remainder of his stale motel coffee and shifted the Buick into drive. Once over the Virginia border, he drove up the steep, winding section of Route 52 that led through Fancy Gap Mountain into Pikesville. When August was ten minutes away, the dot stopped in front of a small diner on Main Street.

The tracker had worked flawlessly. Case's truck was exactly where the device indicated it would be—parallel parked in front of the long white train car that now stood as the Pikesville Diner. According to the app on his phone, the truck had been stationary for about fifteen minutes. Plenty of time for Case to have gotten settled. August parked on the opposite side of the street, purchased a copy of the *Cook County Gazette* from a newspaper vending machine, and walked calmly toward the diner.

The place was much bigger than it looked from the outside. A friendly waitress met August at the door. She wore tight jeans that draped over a pair of battered cowboy boots, a t-shirt, and a short white apron that had her name embroidered across the front—"Peggy."

"Good mornin', sir. Welcome to the Pikesville Diner. You can sit yourself wherever ya like."

"Thank you, Peggy," August replied as he scanned the room. The place was a veritable blue-collar boys club, with an assortment of overall-clad farmers and factory workers, all talking, laughing, and enjoying what looked to be a hearty home-cooked breakfast. August saw Case sitting at a table near the window, but was careful not to make eye contact. He was with the woman and teenage girl Whitlock had listed in the target package as close acquaintances. Aside from Peggy, they looked to be the only two women in the place. August walked to the table closest to Case's and took a seat facing away from his target. Peggy followed with her notepad and pencil in hand.

"What can I get started for ya, sir?"

August slipped on his reading glasses and looked down his nose at the menu, "I'll have a black coffee, a glass of water, two eggs over easy, and a side of...I'm sorry, what's the difference between country ham and city ham?"

"You're gonna want the country ham, sweetie. City ham is milder, like a lot of the store-bought stuff, whereas country ham is salted and dry-cured. That's how we usually prefer it around here."

"I think I'll try the country ham then," August said.

"Okay. Any biscuits or toast with that?"

August glanced around at the plates of the other customers, "Sure. A biscuit sounds great, thank you."

"Peggy scribbled the order on her notepad, "Alrighty then, we'll have that out to ya right away."

The Pikesville Diner had a different vibe than the ones in Chicago. It felt more like a small piece of history had been cut away from the past and plopped down in the center of town, unaffected by the passage of time. August found himself genuinely looking forward to the experience.

Peggy returned with August's water and a pot of hot black coffee. She set a thick porcelain mug on the table and topped it off. "Your breakfast should be right out," she said before she turned to greet more customers coming through the door.

August opened the newspaper while he waited and focused on the conversation happening behind him.

"So, what time do you plan on leaving tomorrow?" The woman asked.

"I'd like to get on the road early. The 81's always a mess, so I'll probably take the 221 as far as I can. It might take longer, but at least I won't be fightin' that traffic."

August continued to eavesdrop as Peggy laid out his breakfast. A large plate of country ham and eggs with a side plate containing two big steaming biscuits.

"I didn't know if you wanted anything with your biscuits, so I brought you some jelly and a side of fresh sausage gravy," Peggy said as she set the smaller bowls off to the side.

"Peggy, this looks fantastic. Thank you again." August said as he admired the piping hot meal in front of him. It made him thankful that Joe had decided to hand the surveillance portion of the job off to him. The kid knew his looks would draw attention in a place like Pikesville, so August would enjoy his big country breakfast while Joe made do with whatever soggy, reheated mess the motel would be serving.

Case and his companions continued their conversation. Mundane bits of information about the farm's upkeep, cattle rotation, and some concerns over a boy named Trevor. Nothing August could use. So, instead of focusing on Case and risking drawing the man's attention, August focused on his food.

There was no rush. August knew when Case was leaving now and roughly what route he would take. That was really all the information he needed. He would pick up a local road map on his way down the mountain and relay what he'd learned to Joe.

Case and the two girls finished their meal and said goodbye to Peggy and a few other customers before leaving. Satisfied with how the morning had turned out, August returned to his salty country ham and thoughts of Maria.

"You coming?" Sam asked as she climbed into the truck behind Mia.

Case stood on the sidewalk staring at the beige Buick parked on the other side of the road. It was a North Carolina rental, but the man driving it had a distinct Chicago accent—not many people came to Pikesville for business trips—a tourist, perhaps? Maybe—but despite all the open tables in the diner, the man had chosen to sit close to Case and Sam, and that got Case's attention.

"Yeah. Sorry." Case said as he walked to the driver's side door and lifted himself into the cab. It was probably nothing, but he made a mental note of the Buick and the man who'd been driving it. After everything that had happened, Case wasn't taking any chances with strangers.

Chapter 17

Joe peered over the embankment and down a steep sandstone cliff face. He'd spent the entire day scouring Route 221 for the right place to make the hit. Augie had marked several points on his map where "accidents" could happen, but there was no way to know for sure without checking firsthand. *This is definitely the spot*, Joe thought. The two-hundred-foot dropoff ended abruptly in a rocky outcropping along the banks of what was labeled Chestnut Creek on the map. There was a wide gravel shoulder on that side of the road, which Joe guessed was a stopping point for tourists wanting a panoramic view of the Blue Ridge Mountains. There was no guardrail, so if he hit Case in the curve, he could run the man's truck into the gravel, causing him to lose traction and careen down the almost vertical slope. *No way anybody could survive that fall.*

Joe climbed back into the Buick and dialed Augie's number. "Okay, I've got it all figured out," he stated confidently when August answered.

"Good. What's next?"

"I need a moving van. Something with some mass but still easy to control. A fifteen-footer should do the trick."

"I can handle that. There's a U-Haul place not half a mile from here."

"Sweet. Park it at the motel. I'll be back in an hour or two. I want to run through this a few more times. We'll pack up and go over the details tonight. Tomorrow, we'll get checked out early and position ourselves for the hit before Case leaves the farm. The tracker's still on his truck, so we'll know when he's moving."

August was impressed with Joe's thoroughness and professionalism. "Good job, Joe. I'll get the moving truck and have it here when you get back. I'll also research drop-off points further north. We'll confirm the deed is done, turn the truck in, link up, and catch flights home from Lynchburg. Sound good?"

"Sounds good, Augie. And hey…" Joe paused until he found the right words. "I won't let you down, okay? I know you want out, and that this is your way of making sure I'm ready to take over. I appreciate you trusting me with it."

August didn't know how a father-son relationship was supposed to feel. He'd never had one with his dad, but this had to be what it was like. August took pride in Joe. He'd nurtured him and watched him grow into his own man. Now, he was ready to turn him loose to make his own way in a business only the strongest could survive. Joe was ready, and so was August.

"You're the *only* person I trust, Joe. You've proven yourself to me time and time again, so I know you can handle it. Take your time and get this right. I'll see you when you get back."

Joe stood there for a while after hanging up, peering across the blue expanse of rolling mountains that stretched out to the horizon. *This has to be flawless*, Joe thought as he opened the "Find My" app on his phone and checked Case's location. He was still at the farm. But come tomorrow, he'd be at the bottom of this ravine, and Joe would be stepping into the shoes of a legend.

Chapter 18

Tanner sat at his desk with his hands folded in front of him as Edwin, the IT specialist he'd brought along, got dressed. The boy was in his early twenties and what most women would consider "cute," but to Tanner, he was nothing more than a handy distraction. Tanner had been in no mood to fuck the boy himself—he'd left that to Hope, the seventeen-year-old intern he'd brought along to keep himself occupied in the event he got bored with Celia. The stress he was under may have kept him from participating, but it was still satisfying to watch and direct. Especially when he knew he could make them do things to each other that no functional couple would ever try. Hope sat on the edge of the couch, half-dressed, looking as if she might cry.

"Jesus, Hope! Would you stop acting like such a fucking prude. You used to suck dick for Ketamine, for God's sake. So don't act like what just happened is somehow appalling to you."

The girl choked out an apology, "I'm sorry, Mr. Greene."

"Just put your clothes on and get the fuck out of my sight, please."

The girl did as she was told and rushed from the office, clutching her blouse. Edwin looked at Tanner and risked speaking on the girl's behalf, "Sir, she's not trying to—"

Tanner's face filled with contempt, "Don't! You're here for the same reason she is—my amusement, so just keep your fucking mouth shut."

Edwin hung his head and was about to leave when Tanner

called him back. "Wait. On second thought, there is something else you can do for me."

The boy turned around but didn't say anything.

"Have the security team show you to the control room. I want you stationed there, monitoring all movement in and around the house. If anything whatsoever looks out of the ordinary, I want to know about it immediately. I have limited resources at the moment, and I need my security team with me, so you're not to leave that room unless someone relieves you. Understood?

"Yes, sir," Edwin said as he obediently turned and walked away.

Once the room was empty, Tanner went back to pacing. His mind raced, wondering how much more pressure he should exert on Whitlock. Fortunately, the senator wasn't the only one Tanner had on video sleeping with underage women. He possessed a trove of evidence against some of the world's most influential people. More than enough information to keep himself out of jail. Granted, most of them didn't know that video proof of what they'd done even existed. They'd either been lied to, coerced, or, in some cases, drugged to get the footage—the fools. What was worrisome was the fact that Case Younger was still out there somewhere. Younger didn't care about the videos or the people involved. He was a singularly focused threat, and Tanner knew he was coming.

Chapter 19

Trevor helped Case carry the last of his gear to the truck and pack it away. After making sure everything was where it should be, the pair started back toward the house so Case could say his final goodbyes and begin his trip north.

"So, you're not sure how long you'll be gone?" Trevor asked.

"Once we reach New York, I doubt it'll take more than two or three days. After that, we'll wrap up the after-action reports, and I'll be right back here. You'll barely know I was gone."

Trevor nodded, "And you'll be working with the same guys who helped you take down JC Wilks?"

Case knew Trevor had handled himself bravely during the incident with Wilks, but didn't want him to worry about what came next. "Yeah, buddy. Those guys have had my back through thick and thin. They'll be right there with me, so I don't need you stressin' over any of that, okay? Besides, you'll have your hands full here with Mia and your grandpa. That should keep you plenty busy."

"And those guys are good at finding people?"

Case looked at Trevor, "They're the best. Why?"

Trevor didn't say anything further, but Case could see the boy had something else on his mind. "You okay?"

"Yeah. I'm fine. We'll just miss ya, is all."

Case put his arm around Trevor, and the two continued toward the house in silence.

Sam, Mia, and Dimpsey were waiting on the porch when they walked around the corner.

"You all ready to go?" Sam asked.

"Just about. I just need to grab my gun from inside, then I'll head out."

"Your brother said to make sure you stop by the station. He wants to see you before you leave." She added.

"I will. I know him and Amanda are leaving for their honeymoon, so I'll be sure to stop."

Trevor spoke up from the foot of the steps, "Hey, I promised my friend, Billy, that I'd pick him up and drive him to practice today, so I'm gonna have to go. I wish I could see ya off, Case, but I'm late as it is. I'll be here when ya come home, okay?"

"Okay, pal. I'll see ya when I get back." Case said as he watched Trevor walk away.

Dimpsey shrugged and shook his head. "Mia, is Trevor okay?"

"He's fine. Just a little sad that Case is goin' away. I'll go check on him." Mia said as she wrapped her arms around Case and squeezed him tightly. "Bye, Case. Be safe, alright? I love you."

"I love you too, sweetheart. I'll see ya soon."

Mia let go and ran around the corner of the house after Trevor.

"Well," Dimpsey said, "I suppose I'll leave you two in peace. Keep your head on straight, and don't let any of those fools get the drop on ya. We'll all be waitin' here when ya come home." Dimpsey shook Case's hand and tried to mask the emotion on his face, "You be careful, son."

Case felt his throat tighten. "I will, Dimpsey."

The old man stepped reluctantly off the porch as if there were more he wanted to say, but he straightened his back and started toward home, leaving Case and Sam alone.

"That man loves you like his own son, you know that, don't you?" Sam said, standing next to Case.

"I know." Case replied as he watched his old friend walk down the long gravel driveway. Once Dimpsey was out of sight, Case turned and walked into the house, too overcome by his feelings to say anything else.

"You need to hurry," Mia cautioned as Trevor climbed into the back of Case's truck.

"I know. Here, hold this," Trevor said, handing his backpack to Mia through the back hatch.

With the camper top installed, he didn't have enough space to stand, so, as best he could on his knees, Trevor shifted Case's deployment bags and gearboxes around to make himself a place to hide. Once satisfied with his work, Trevor returned to the opening and grabbed his backpack from Mia, who was starting to panic.

"Jesus, Trevor, what if you get caught?"

Trevor grinned and tried reassuring Mia that his plan would work, "It's only a little over five hours. I'll just crawl into my little hole here and take a nap. We'll be in McLean by the time I wake up."

Mia shook her head, "And what happens when you get there? You'll just pop out the back like a jack-in-the-box. Surprise, Case! Look who tagged along."

Trevor knew Mia was right. He hadn't really thought that far ahead but had faith that Case would understand his situation and be willing to help.

"I'll figure that part out when we get there. But I don't need you worrying like this and giving anything away before we even get out of the driveway."

Mia looked hurt. "I'm just worried about you, is all. You can't be mad at me for that."

Trevor realized that in his rush to leave, he'd been insensitive to Mia's feelings. "Hey." He said, leaning his head out into the open air. "I'm sorry. This has all been really hard, and knowing that my mom might be out there somewhere…this is just somethin' I have to do. Okay? I can't focus on what Case, Grandpa, or anybody else thinks about it."

Mia nodded and glanced over her shoulder to hide the tears in her eyes, "I understand. Okay, you need to hide. Case'll probably be out here any minute."

Trevor could see she was still hurting, so he did the only thing he knew to do and kissed her full on the lips. Mia pressed her fingers into Trevor's thick brown hair and kissed him back, but broke it off before she started begging him to stay.

"Be careful, Trevor Campbell."

"I will, Mia Raines. And I'll be back here to finish that kiss. Okay?"

Mia smiled and closed the hatch. Her job now would be to take Trevor's truck to the ballfield and keep it out of sight until Case was gone. As she walked to the big gray Dodge 2500 that Case had given Trevor, the thought occurred to her that this had been their first farewell kiss, but probably not their last. If Trevor was going to follow in Case's footsteps, saying goodbye was just something she'd probably need to get used to.

Case stood at the gun safe in his closet and prepped his Glock 19 for the trip. He dropped the magazine into his palm and made sure it was topped off before checking the chamber—sixteen rounds total. After reinserting the mag and snapping the weapon into its Q-Series Stealth holster, Case slid the weapon into the one o'clock position behind his belt and stuck an extra magazine into his left front pocket. Before closing the safe door, Case looked up to see his dad's 1970 .38 Detective Special lying on the top shelf. Avis had won the pistol in a poker game just before getting out of the Army. Case remembered his dad carrying the nickel-plated Colt everywhere he went. He never really understood why back then. When he asked his dad about it, Avis simply answered, "Son, it's better to have it and not need it than it is to need it and not have it." Case couldn't explain why, but he felt compelled to take the old revolver with him. "*It's better to have it and not need it, I suppose,*" he thought to himself as he grabbed the shiny, snub-nosed pistol and shoved it into his waistband. A chill crept up his spine as the cold steel frame touched the bare skin of his back. Case shook the feeling off, locked the safe, and walked outside to say his final goodbye to Sam.

Chapter 20
Pikesville, Virginia
1997

Tina Scott was enjoying high school. There had been a few disciplinary issues during her freshman and sophomore years. Still, for the most part, Tina got along well with the other kids in her class and maintained a B average on her report cards. Her mom kept mostly to herself and stayed busy with her job at the furniture factory, sanding bedposts. In the absence of friends or family around the house, Tina found work as a checkout girl at the local Food Lion, where she was striking up a relationship with one of the stock boys, James Campbell.

James was intelligent and hard-working. It didn't hurt that he was also tall and handsome. His dad, Dimpsey Campbell, ran the hardware store in town and owned some property. Vera always joked that since the man was a widower, perhaps she should pay him a visit herself, which Tina thought was gross and wildly inappropriate. One day, just as Tina was about to clock out and go home, James approached her with his apron in his hand.

"Hey, James."

"Hi Tina," The boy responded shyly.

Tina tucked a strand of curly black hair behind her ear and smiled, "What's going on with you today? Is everything okay?"

"Yeah," the boy said, doing his best to act casual. Realizing that he'd left his Mustangs baseball cap on, James quickly reached up and jerked the hat from his head, revealing a head full of wild brown hair. He combed through it with his fingers, trying to tame it, but his hair had other plans. Tina giggled.

James gave up and got to the point. "I was just wondering if anybody had asked you to the sweethearts dance yet. It's next Thursday, and I figured if no one else had asked you, maybe we could go together."

Tina blushed. No one had ever asked her out before, and the fact that James Campbell was the first put an enormous grin on her face. "I'd love to go to the dance with you, James. I'll have to check with my mom first and get a dress and everything, but yeah. That'll be fun."

James tried to play it cool but found it impossible to hide his excitement. "That's awesome! Okay then," he said as he twisted the ball cap in his hands like a wet dishrag. "I'm looking forward to it."

Tina couldn't help but fall instantly in love with the boy, "Me too, James."

The store manager, Nora, caught the interaction and decided to break it up. "Alright, you two. Get to work, or I'm docking your pay."

She wouldn't, of course, but the last thing customers needed to see when they walked in was two love-struck teenagers standing at the entrance on the verge of making out.

"Yes, ma'am," they both shouted in unison before returning to work. Tina still had thirty minutes left in her shift, so she returned to her register just as Mrs. Beasley started loading what looked like a cart full of cat food onto the conveyor. As she rang up the individual cans and stacked them into a brown paper bag, her mind was anywhere but on her job. She glanced over to see James smiling at her from the corner of the bread aisle as he loaded packs of hot dog buns onto the shelves. Tina smiled back and did her best to focus, but cat food was the last thing on her mind. She couldn't wait to clock out and get home to tell her mom the news.

Chapter 21
Present Day

A light rain dampened the windshield as Case passed the Cook County Line into the town of Sawyers Mill, Virginia. He flipped the wipers on, then slowly spun the knob on the truck's old Mopar radio until he found a local news station. After a few commercials and some high school baseball scores, Case learned that the weather would only worsen the further north he went. No big deal. He had the camper top on now, so he wasn't worried about anything getting wet. Case twisted the knob again and landed on his favorite classic country station, 98.1 WBRF—the same station he and Bobby would listen to as kids when Avis would drive them into town. The steady, rhythmic drumming of the wiper blades coupled with the soothing tones of Patsy Cline coming through the dashboard speakers lulled Case's mind into complete emptiness, a luxury he seldom allowed himself.

It was the Buick that snapped him out of it. Case was staring out over one of the broad mountain vistas along the 221 when he spotted the beige sedan parked on the side of the road. An older man with short gray hair sat in the driver's seat, talking on his phone. Case thought nothing of it at first, so by the time it registered in his mind that he'd seen both the car and the man before, it was too late. Case turned his attention back to the road just as a large white moving van crossed over the center line into his lane halfway through a blind curve.

With limited options, Case jerked the wheel hard right to avoid a head-on collision. But in doing so, the old Power

Wagon hit gravel and slipped into a skid. Case's mind subconsciously raced through a series of counter-steering techniques he'd picked up during his Foreign Affairs Counter Threat Training in Glynco, Georgia. Reflexively, Case's right foot came off the gas as his left hammered down on the clutch. He forced himself to look away from the ravine and back at the road where he needed to go. As the truck's rear end slid to the left, Case turned the steering wheel in the same direction, then corrected right again to straighten up. He quickly determined that the only way to stop himself from plummeting over the edge was to hit a large boulder sitting at the far end of the pull-off, hoping the impact would bounce him back toward the pavement. Case locked his eyes on the massive stone and started to brake as he continued making minor adjustments in his steering. The heavy steel brush guard Avis had installed years ago clipped the corner of the rock and spun Case around. With the front tires now facing the road, he let off the clutch and pressed hard on the gas until the truck gained traction, pulling him away from the cliff. Once he knew he was clear, Case slammed on the brakes and slid to a halt. Both hands gripped the steering wheel so hard he could feel the blood pulsing in his palms. When he glanced out the driver-side window, he saw that he was only a few feet from the drop-off. A fall from that height would have killed him for sure. Case let out a sigh of relief and looked around for the moving van, which he now saw speeding up the road. Clearly, the guy had no intention of stopping.

"Asshole." Case mumbled to himself.

He sat quietly for a while, letting the adrenaline work its way out of his system. His hands started to shake uncontrollably, so he forced himself to breathe deeply, over and over again, until his heart rate stabilized and the trembling subsided. In the calmness that followed, Case heard something moving behind him, then a voice.

"Jesus Christ, Case! What the hell happened?"

Stunned, Case jerked his head around to see the familiar form of Trevor Campbell as he crawled shakily from the truck bed and fell haphazardly into the mud, thankful to be alive.

Part Two
Conflict

Chapter 22

"Fuck!" Joe smashed his fists against the steering wheel as he watched Case's truck careen toward the drop-off, then bounce off a large boulder and stop just short of the cliff's edge. After all the meticulous preparation, his plan had failed, and Joe was taking it personally. As he sped past the beige sedan on the side of the road, his phone rang in the cupholder beside him. It was August, and he dreaded the man's reaction.

"What happened? I just saw you drive past. Is it done?"

Joe's voice was tense, "The plan didn't work, Augie. Younger was able to recover and keep from going over."

"Where is he now?" August asked, "Is he still mobile?"

"I'm not sure. It had to have shaken him up, so if he is mobile, I doubt he'll follow me, but I need to ditch this truck, quick."

August was quiet for a while, "Okay. We'll have to figure something else out, but for now, just get to the U-Haul place. I'll pick you up there, and we can regroup."

"I'm sorry, Augie. There's no way he should have been able to survive that. I don't know what happened."

"You said it yourself, Joe. This guy isn't some clueless corporate whistleblower. He's playing on a different level. The good news is, as far as he knows, that was just some asshole not paying attention that ran him off the road. If the tracker is still on the truck and working the way it should, we can come at him again. I'll figure it out, okay. Don't beat yourself up."

Joe didn't know how to respond. It wasn't like August to

be so casual about a missed hit. In most cases, he'd be losing his shit right now, but something in the old man had changed. Maybe it was knowing that this was his last job. Or perhaps he was just losing his edge; either way, the hit was still Joe's responsibility.

"Okay, Augie. I'll see ya at the rental place." Joe hung up and slipped the phone into his shirt pocket. His head started to throb as his mind raced through the litany of problems a missed hit could cause—heightened awareness of the target and exposure of the people who had ordered the hit. Neither of those things were good, but the latter concerned Joe the most. If Whitlock became exposed, there's no way he'd keep his mouth shut. He was a politician, after all. The guy would flip the story to place the blame on August, then once August was locked away, the senator would have him killed on the inside to tie up loose ends. The thought occurred to Joe that if he failed again, this wouldn't just be August's last job. It could be his as well. After everything Augie had done for him, there was no way he'd let the man pay for his mistake. He'd disappointed a lot of people in his lifetime, but the man who'd treated him like a son had never been one of them. He'd see this thing finished no matter what it took.

Still shaken by the accident, Case jumped from his truck and helped Trevor to his feet.

"Jesus Christ, Trevor. What the hell are you doing? Are you okay?"

Trevor twisted his neck left and right, then tried to focus on Case, who held him by the shoulders.

After a thorough inspection, Case was amazed to find the

boy uninjured. "Trevor, look at me. What are you doing in the back of my truck? Why are you here?"

"Trevor shook his head forcefully to clear it. "Case, I—" He started, but was still too frazzled to continue.

"It's alright, kid. Let's just get you back home, okay?"

Trevor pulled away and stepped back, "No, Case. I can't."

"What?" Case was confused. "Why can't you go back?"

Trevor placed both hands on his knees, took a deep breath, and then forced himself upright to look Case in the eyes. "Because. Mom's alive, Case. Wilks told me so before he died. He was the only man who knew how to find her. Now he's dead. I was hoping that if I could make it up to McLean, you and your friends could help me track her down. You said that's what they do."

Case turned toward the hazy expanse of mountains that stretched beyond the cliff face and exhaled slowly. "He told you Tina was alive?"

Trevor hung his head. "He said he knew where she was. The only chance I have of finding her now is you."

"So, this is why you've been keeping your distance lately? You could have talked to me, ya know?"

"I was afraid you'd take Grandpa's side and shut me down."

"Your grandpa'll kill me if he thinks I had any part in this." Case said, turning back to Trevor.

"Maybe he won't be so upset if you talk to him. This is important to me, Case."

There was a tense silence. Trevor thought Case would say no and take him straight back to Pikesville. But after a moment, Case seemed to relax.

"Okay." Case thought of losing his own mother and how much it would have meant to him at that age to speak to her again. He could see the pain in the boy's face and couldn't bring himself to say no. "Here's my offer. There's a motel up the road close to the interstate. Let's go there and get you cleaned up. I'll call your grandpa and explain things. But the final decision will be his. If he says no, I take you straight home, no questions asked. Agreed?"

"Agreed," Trevor replied with more than a hint of resignation in his voice.

"Good, now get in the truck, and let's get off the side of this damned mountain."

"Sounds good to me," Trevor said, wiping mud and dirt from his jeans.

"And please sit in the front this time."

Chapter 23

"He did what?" Dimpsey growled into the phone. Case knew that his friend was upset, especially after he'd told him about the accident, but the anger soon subsided and was replaced by the frightened concern of a loving grandfather.

"He's okay, isn't he?"

"He's fine. Just a few bumps and bruises, but nothing serious."

"I mean about his mom. Is he okay? I hate that the boy didn't come to me with this."

"I know, and I told him he should have, but he was afraid we'd try to stop him."

"Damn boy's as stubborn as his daddy was."

"Maybe even as stubborn as his grandpa." Case quipped, trying to ease the tension.

"Don't be a smartass, Case. I'm in no mood."

Case knew Dimpsey couldn't see him, but wiped the smile from his face anyway.

"So, what do you want me to do? He's not concussed, but he could probably use a little time to get his head right. The brush guard saved the truck, so I'm still mobile. We're parked at a motel just outside Christiansburg right now. I can wait for you here while he settles down, or I can get him cleaned up and bring him back home. It's up to you."

Dimpsey was silent for a while. "How far away is McLean from here?" He asked.

"A little over five hours if you stick to the interstate."

"Okay. You and Trevor settle in for the night. I'll pack up and leave first thing in the morning and meet you in McLean."

Now, it was Case's turn to be shocked. "Dimpsey, are you sure? I can just bring him back to Pikesville in the morning. It wouldn't put me that far behind schedule. The guys up north will understand."

Dimpsey let out a resigned sigh, "I'm sure, Case. I can't blame the boy for wanting to track down his mother, but he might not like what he finds. If he wants to do this, I need to be there for him. You get him to McLean, and I'll be there right behind ya."

"You're a good man, Dimpsey."

"Debatable," the old man muttered. "Let me speak to the boy if you think he's up to it."

Case handed the phone over to Trevor, who sat on the truck's passenger seat, suddenly looking more terrified than he had after the accident.

"Here ya go, kid."

"Grandpa, I—" Trevor started, but was cut off immediately.

"Don't speak, Trevor. Just listen."

Trevor did as he was told.

"Trevor, let me start by sayin' I'm sorry."

The boy was surprised to hear an apology but knew better than to interrupt.

"I know you've been strugglin' lately, and I just turned a blind eye to it, thinkin' you'd snap out of it. That was wrong of me."

"It's okay, Grandpa. I should have talked to you first." Trevor responded.

"I understand why you didn't. I know I can be ill-tempered sometimes, and that you think I still look at you as just a kid or somethin'. But the truth is, you ain't much younger than I was when I got shipped off to Vietnam. If I made it through that, I'm sure you can make it through this just fine. But I don't want you to do it by yourself, okay?"

"I was hoping Case's buddies could help me out. He said that's what they do. They find people."

"They do, but I think they might have their hands full with this, Greene guy. So, here's what we're gonna do. Case'll stay with ya tonight, get you cleaned up and settled. Ya'll are gonna head north in the morning. Once you get to McLean, I'll meet you there. Case and his team can go do what they need to do, and I can help you track your mother down. Fair enough?"

Trevor couldn't find the right words to express his feelings, so he stuck with the simplest ones he could think of, "Thanks, Grandpa."

"I've raised you like my own son, and I'd never turn my back on you, but I need to warn you about something."

"About what?"

"Your mother isn't exactly who you think she is, Trevor."

"What does that mean?"

"I mean, you remember your mom a certain way. You have this version of her in your head that's based on old pictures and stories I've told, and for the most part, that's her. She loved you very much, but she also had a pretty dark past. One that came back to haunt her. I just don't want you to be disappointed by what you might find."

Trevor's voice filled with emotion. "I just need to know, Grandpa. I need to know why she left and what's keepin' her from coming back. I could use your help."

Dimpsey cleared his throat to keep it from cracking, "I've always been on your side, Trevor. So, from now on, me and you are a team, just like Case and his buddies, alright?"

"Okay, Grandpa. I love you."

Dimpsey swallowed hard, "I love you too, son."

The line went dead, and Trevor handed the phone back to Case.

"You good, kid?"

"Yeah. I'm good." Trevor said.

Case knew Trevor was doing his best not to cry. It was such an awkward age, that hazy middle ground between boy and man. But in Trevor's case, the man was starting to take more control. "Okay, pal. Let's get ourselves a room and get you cleaned up."

Chapter 24

Tanner sat behind his desk, struggling to come up with a solution to the mess he was in. He hated feeling so vulnerable to outside forces. If Whitlock's man couldn't stop Younger, his only option would be to fight, and he didn't like thinking about how that might end. Tanner stopped himself before his thoughts turned morbid. He needed something else to do—an outlet for his frustrations. Just as he was about to call Celia in to release the stress, his phone rang. Tanner looked down to see Senator Whitlock's name broadcast across the tiny screen, *finally,* he thought, taking a deep breath to calm his nerves before answering. The last thing he wanted now was to show any sign of weakness in front of a man like Whitlock.

"It's about time," Greene answered.

Glen Whitlock didn't waste a moment with small talk. "Tell me what you want, Tanner."

A sly smile spread across Greene's round face. At least now he knew the video he'd sent had made its point. "I need to know what's being done about the Case Younger problem."

Glen simplified his answer as if explaining something complicated to a small child, "I have men taking care of the situation as we speak."

"And? Have they made any progress? When will it be done?"

"Tanner. We don't ask those kinds of questions. These men are professionals. I give them the assignment, and they handle the problem. I usually don't know the deed is done until I see it on the news. It's better that way."

"If Case reaches Athens, it'll be too late. He'll have the support of the Joint Task Force, and I will not be marched out of my own home in handcuffs. I won't allow myself to be humiliated in that way, not alone. Do you understand me? If that happens, you'll go down right beside me."

Whitlock knew Greene wasn't bluffing. Tanner had the Senator by the balls and wouldn't hesitate to tear them off if it meant saving his own ass, "Don't worry about that. The man who runs the Critical Missions Project answers only to the director of the FBI, who happens to be a close personal friend of mine. I'll contact the director myself to shut the whole thing down. That'll at least keep the government off your back while my men handle Case."

Tanner was satisfied with the Senator's compliance, "Good. I'll trust your men to do their jobs and expect to hear directly from you if anything changes."

"You can count on it."

Tanner relaxed, "Very well. Goodbye, Senator."

Glen Whitlock hung up his phone. Hopefully, calling off Andre Brown and the CMP would eliminate any chance of the federal government uncovering the sex tape Tanner was hanging over his head. His best bet now would be to exercise some restraint and wait to hear from his man. Once Younger was eliminated, perhaps Mr. White would be up for a quick trip to Athens, New York, and one more tax-exempt payday funded by the hard-working Americans he represented. Tanner Greene was becoming a problem that needed to be dealt with.

Celia heard Tanner hang up the phone and rushed into the other room so she wouldn't be caught eavesdropping. She knew what kind of man Tanner was and some of what he'd been up to. That night before they left the city, he'd received a phone call that sent him into a panic. Now, Celia knew that people were after Tanner, and the thought of him going away brought her a sense of hope. She didn't know what would happen next, but knew she needed to inform the other staff of the possibilities. She didn't care what it was—a raid, an arrest, an execution—all Celia knew was that Tanner Greene was scared and that she'd do anything she could to assist in his demise.

Chapter 25

BG's Bar and Grill had only been open a few hours, and already, two early morning drinkers sat at the bar swapping stories while Prissy and Sam carried cases of beer up from the basement. Crystal, Sam's best friend and backup bartender, couldn't offer much help. Her leg had been fractured by a stray bullet fired at Bobby's wedding, and she'd been immobile for the past week, but the boredom of being left home alone was more than she could handle. So, she sat at one of the low tables by the bar with her bandaged leg stretched across an empty chair, topping off the salt and pepper shakers. Crystal had been working at Sam's place for a while now, but Prissy was a new addition to the team and more than willing to help while Crystal recovered. After JC had been killed, Prissy, who'd been used as a pawn in his plot against Case, decided to stay in Pikesville and get a fresh start. Sam had offered to let her stay in the house her uncle had left her until the girl felt comfortable enough to strike out on her own. Soon after, Crystal moved in with Prissy to help cover the rent, which Sam found amusing. She would have gladly let Prissy stay for free, so it was obvious to her that the two women were becoming more than just friends. It warmed her heart to see them both so happy. Just as the last case of beer was heaved onto the bar, Dimpsey Campbell came walking through the door.

Sam was stunned to see the man, "Dimpsey, what in the world are you doin' here? Shouldn't you be at the hardware store?"

Dimpsey didn't say anything, but the look on his face let Sam know that something was very wrong. She stopped cold and looked Dimpsey in the eyes, "Dimpsey, what happened?"

Dimpsey knew Sam's mind would instantly go to Case, so he was quick to respond. "Now, don't go worrying yourself about Case. He's fine."

"What happened?" Sam asked again.

"It's Trevor. I just got a call from Case, and it turns out the boy stowed away in the back of his truck to go with him to McLean. There was a minor accident, and Case got run off the road. But, like I said, everyone's fine. That's how Case found Trevor. I promised him I'd stop by here first and tell ya'll what happened before I left."

Sam walked around the bar and pulled a chair from the table beside Crystal, "Jesus. Please, sit down a minute, Dimpsey. Why on earth was Trevor trying to go to McLean with Case? And why wouldn't he tell anybody?"

"Oh, he told somebody. I'm sure of it," Dimpsey said as he sat down.

"Mia," Sam groaned.

"She ran interference while Trevor made his getaway. But I don't want you to be upset with Mia. This is my fault."

"How do you figure?"

"When that asshole, JC, had Trevor, he told the boy that he knew how to find his mother."

"Tina? Are you serious?"

"Yeah. I assumed she was dead when she took off after James's funeral and never came back. You saw how she got—erratic, hiding things, and running around with Rex Kelley and his gang. Nobody ever expected she'd turn up again."

Sam thought back to the night Rex had beaten her senseless and taken Mia. The memory still sent a chill through her blood.

"And JC said she was alive? How would he know?"

"Because, when Tina left, she left with Rex. JC was part of that gang too. If anybody knew how to find her, it would have been him. Trevor decided to take matters into his own hands. He thought if he could make it to McLean, it would be too late to send him home. He figured once he was there, he could talk Case and his friends into helping him track her down."

"So, what now?"

"I've closed the hardware store for the week. I'm gonna pack up and leave in the morning. Case and Trevor will stay in a motel outside Christiansburg for the night. I'll link up with them in McLean tomorrow evening."

"Will it be safe? Letting Trevor wander around looking for his mother?"

"That's why I'm going. Case agreed to ask his boss for help. Hopefully, we can use some of their resources to track Tina down. I just hope the boy understands what he might be getting himself into."

Sam had known Tina and knew she could be impulsive and unpredictable. "She always had a bit of a wild side, and I know her and James had their share of problems. But if finding her is what Trevor needs to do, then I'm glad you're letting him do it."

Dimpsey stood to leave and nodded toward Crystal and Prissy. "We'll see how it goes. You ladies keep an eye on things while I'm away."

"We got ya covered, Dimpsey," Crystal yelled as Sam walked the man to the door and watched him march across the parking lot to his truck. Something about how he moved seemed off, like he was carrying a weight he wasn't accustomed to. Sam breathed deeply and walked back inside. She'd most certainly have a talk with Mia about her role in all this, but as long as everyone was okay, she wouldn't let herself worry. If anyone could help Trevor find his mother, it was Dimpsey Campbell.

Chapter 26
New York, New York
2001

Tina woke to the blare of her alarm clock and sat up in a daze. She rubbed her eyes and looked around to find her roommate, Cynthia, sprawled across the fold-out couch with her latest boyfriend, Rod, surrounded by empty beer cans. Tina slipped out of bed and crept quietly into the bathroom. She didn't know why she was trying so hard to be quiet. Cynthia could sleep through a train wreck when she was like this. Tina brushed her teeth and pulled her jet-black curls into a ponytail as she left for her morning walk around the park. She enjoyed the solitude of these early hours. It relaxed her mind and gave her a little time to think. During her freshman year, she'd always use her alone time to call James before he left for work. But lately, it seemed those calls were getting farther and farther apart. Tina missed him and decided she wanted to hear his voice, so she fished the chunky black phone from the pocket of her sweatpants, flipped it open, and hit speed dial 1.

"Hello." A sleepy voice answered.

"Hey, James."

James's voice shifted quickly from sleepiness to excitement, "Hey, Tina! It's good to hear from ya. You doin' okay?"

"Yeah, I'm good. Just missing home, I suppose."

James wanted to be sympathetic, but Tina had been the one who insisted on going to school so far away from Pikesville. "New York's quite a ways off. I feel like we barely see you anymore."

Tina knew he was right. She could have gone to Tech instead and been only an hour from Pikesville, but the allure of going to college in a big city was too much for her to ignore. "I'll be home this summer like I always am. How are things going at the hardware store?"

"It's good. I like working with Dad. If everything works out, I'll take over in a few years, and he can retire."

"Dimpsey doesn't seem like the retiring type."

"Oh, trust me, he's thinking about it. There's a pile of fly-fishing magazines beside his recliner to prove it."

Tina laughed, "Good for him."

James was quiet for a while, but Tina knew what was coming next. "Have you been seeing anybody?"

They'd agreed when she left that a long-distance relationship would be challenging for both of them, so they'd take a break and see how things went.

"No. You?"

"Of course not," James insisted.

Things had been so different in high school. Tina loved James and felt happy with him, but there was a restlessness inside her that she couldn't explain—some pull toward a different life. She didn't know exactly what she wanted—just something different. The idea of taking a break had been more hers than his, and she knew the decision bothered James. Now, the conversation would turn awkward and forced, as it always did, so Tina decided to end it.

"I know you have to get ready for work, so I'll let you go, okay? I do miss you."

James took a deep breath, "I miss you too. I guess I'll see ya this summer?"

"Sure," Tina said as she looked out over Central Park, feeling further from Pikesville than she ever had. "Bye, James."

"Bye, Tina."

When Tina got back to the dorm room, Cynthia and Rod were awake.

Cynthia greeted Tina in her usual style. "Hey Bitch. What are you getting into tonight?"

"Nothing, really. I planned on doing some laundry later, but—"

"Hell no. You're not spending your Saturday night washing clothes." Cynthia cocked her head toward Rod, who was getting dressed and having a hard time finding his balance. "You're coming out with us tonight."

"Okay, where are we going?"

Rod spoke up from the couch as he laced up his shoes. "My friend Donnie's throwing a rager on the Lower East Side. It's gonna be fuckin nuts."

Tina knew the kind of parties Rod and Cynthia went to. A part of her was afraid and wanted to say no. But she also felt that irresistible pull into the excitement of something new, and that was a feeling she seldom ignored.

"Sounds like a good time. Count me in."

Chapter 27
Present Day

Despite its name, the Blue Mountain Lodge sat nestled in a low valley just north of Christiansburg, Virginia. The rooms were cheap but tidy and its placement offered easy access to the interstate and a few local restaurants. Trevor sat in the truck, fruitlessly thumbing through search results for his mother, while Case went inside to secure a room. When he returned, Trevor looked discouraged.

"You okay, kid?"

"Yeah. I'm good. It's just frustrating. It's like mom never existed."

Case smiled, "Not everybody's online, buddy. Besides, Google's not gonna tell ya what you need to know. Once we make it to McLean, you'll have a lot more resources and support on your side. I promise."

Trevor put his phone away. "You got us a room?"

"I did." Case closed the driver's side door, pulled across the narrow parking lot, and backed the truck in a few spaces down from room number 12. "Stay put for a second and keep an eye on the lobby for me."

Before Trevor could say anything, Case was out of the truck and walking down the covered sidewalk. He turned left, stopped in front of room 15, and looked around. Trevor saw him pull something from his pocket and squat to bring himself level with the doorknob. After a few seconds of tinkering with the lock, Case opened the door to room 15 and walked back to the truck. "Okay, kid. Grab your stuff and get inside."

Case had a *don't ask any questions* look on his face, so Trevor kept quiet. As Case grabbed his duffle and another equipment bag from the back, Trevor pulled his backpack from the floorboard and did as he was told.

They slipped quickly into the room. Case closed the door behind Trevor, locked it with both the deadbolt and security chain, then pulled the drapes shut. Trevor stared from the corner, as Case unzipped his duffle and pulled out a small rubber wedge, placed it on the ground, and kicked it underneath the door. It was a trick he'd picked up when he worked as a Federal Air Marshal, and it had proven useful on more than one occasion. Case also looked around the small bathroom and checked the locks on the windows. When he walked back in, he seemed a little less on edge.

"Case…Is everything okay?" Trevor asked as he pitched his backpack onto one of the small twin beds.

Case peered through the curtains and scanned the parking lot one more time, grabbed a small wooden chair, and moved it closer to the window.

"I'm just being cautious, kid."

"But why? The guy you're after is all the way up in New York."

Case's eyes turned cold. "Trevor. I get the feeling that what happened earlier today wasn't an accident. And the guy I'm after isn't the type of person who fights his own battles, so we have to be careful."

Trevor looked surprised, "Really? You think that van tried to run us off the road on purpose?"

Case shook his head. "I'm not positive, but just before the accident, I passed a car sitting on the side of the road."

"And?"

"And I recognized the car and the man driving it from the Pikesville diner yesterday morning. With everything that's happened in the last year, I don't put a lot of stock in coincidences. I'm just being cautious."

Trevor glanced around and noticed the room key lying on a small laminate table in the corner. The yellow tag attached to it had the number twelve printed clearly in the center.

"Case, did you break into this room?"

Case looked over at Trevor, "Yeah, I did. Never let them find ya where they expect ya to be, kid. Always keep 'em guessing."

"What if someone checks in tonight?"

"There was a sign hanging in the lobby when I booked the room. Something about construction work. I asked the girl working the desk about it. She said the motel doesn't get many guests, so they're remodeling all the odd-numbered rooms. We'll be safe here tonight."

"Why did you pick this one?"

Because the motel is shaped like an "L". This room looks directly out to room 12, where everybody thinks we'll be. Plus, it's close enough to the truck that we could slip out and make a getaway if we need to."

"So, what do we do now?"

"Well, you're gonna go shower and wash the mud off yourself. After that, you'll get a good night's rest, and I'll sit here at the window to keep watch."

"Won't you need to sleep too?"

Case turned his attention back to the parking lot, "Don't worry about me. I'll be fine."

Luckily, the tracker hadn't been dislodged during the accident. August and Joe had followed the tiny blue blip on the phone to a small roadside motel that looked practically abandoned. August pulled the Buick into a gas station across the street and parked. Through the trees, they could see Case's truck in the motel parking lot along with three other cars. They figured one of those probably belonged to the attendant on duty. That meant most of the rooms would be empty. August cut the headlights to the Buick as he pulled in so he wouldn't alert anyone to their arrival.

Augie looked over at Joe and nodded. Joe tapped the screen on his phone and dialed the motel's number. A young female voice answered on the second ring.

"Blue Mountain Lodge. How may I help you?"

"Hey, ma'am," Joe said, sounding as sad as possible. "My brother is staying with you guys tonight and…Well, there's no easy way to say this. Our father just passed away and—"

"Oh, my goodness, honey. I'm so sorry to hear that." The girl interrupted.

"I know my brother'll take it hard, and I didn't want to tell him over the phone. I'm only about twenty minutes away, and I was wondering if you could give me his room number. I'd like to tell him face to face so neither of us has to be alone."

"Of course, sweetie. What's your brother's name?"

"It's Younger, ma'am. Case Younger."

"Of course. Your brother just checked into room 12 not long ago. I'm really so sorry to hear about ya'lls Daddy."

"It's okay. He was old and had a full life. I appreciate your help," Joe said as he hung up the phone and looked at August with a smile.

"You went a little cold there at the end, didn't ya, pal?"

"What the hell. We got the room number. I'm not wanting to drag this out, so let's just go get it done."

"Don't be in such a rush, Joe. Case just checked in, we'll give him time to settle in and relax. We have him cornered, so let's take our time and do this right."

Joe sat back and looked across the parking lot at the motel. He knew he'd blown his shot earlier, and now Augie was taking the lead again. But something felt off. August didn't have the same drive or focus that he used to, and it concerned Joe. He didn't know what had changed, but all he could do now was sit quietly and wait.

"Okay, Augie. We go when you say go."

Chapter 28

It was almost three in the morning when Case spotted two men walking cautiously from across the street. They stuck to the shadows, but in the dim light of the overhead lamps, Case recognized one of them as the man he'd seen parked on the side of the road just before the accident. The same one he'd seen at the diner. Case didn't have a clear visual on the other man, but could make out the faint silhouette of a pistol held tightly in his right hand. It was time to go.

Case rushed across the room and shook Trevor, who woke with a start, "Let's go. It's time to leave."

Trevor sat up on the edge of the bed and rubbed his eyes. "What? What's happening?"

Case unzipped the long, OD green bag he had lying on the bed and removed his Daniel Defense MK18 Short-Barrel Rifle and body armor. He slapped a thirty-round mag into the mag well, racked the charging handle, and slung the ballistic vest over his chest.

"No time for questions, Trevor. We have to move. Now!"

Trevor jumped out of bed, fully dressed. Case had insisted that he sleep in his clothes. Now he knew why. Case pitched Trevor's backpack to him from across the room and slid the SBR's adjustable two-point sling over his shoulder.

"Put that on and grab my duffle. When I step outside this door, you get behind me and hold onto my belt. You don't let go until we get to the truck. Got it?"

Trevor nodded, and his face went pale.

"We've got about twenty yards of open ground to cover. Be quick. Be quiet." Case said, looking Trevor in the eyes.

Trevor nodded again without speaking. Case removed the rubber wedge from the door, tucked it into his pocket, and twisted the deadbolt. Once he felt Trevor's grip tighten around his belt, Case cracked the door open, raised the SBR to his shoulder, and stepped calmly through the breach.

The door to room 12 stood open, and Case could see lights swinging left and right as the men inside searched for their target. In a crouch, he continued toward the truck, never taking his eyes or his sights off the open door. Just as he reached the truck, the gray-haired man from the diner stepped out into the parking lot and looked Case dead in the eyes. Then he raised his gun.

Everything started to move in slow motion for Case. He could see the man's face shift from shocked to resolute as he brought his pistol to bear, but it was too late for him. Case already had him in his sights and pulled the trigger. Case felt Trevor jump behind him at the sound of three sharp pops. He swung the passenger side door open and stepped forward, giving Trevor room to climb inside.

"In. Now!"

Trevor sprang into the passenger seat and slammed the door closed behind him as Case backed away and moved toward the front of the truck, using the engine block as cover. The second man appeared in the open doorway. He was skinny and tattooed and had the merciless glare of a man accustomed to killing. Case fired again, sending the man diving for cover, and kept firing until he was at the driver's side door. He lifted himself into the old Power Wagon and cranked it just as the tattooed man reappeared and started shooting back. Case could hear the hollow thump of rounds impacting the heavy steel tailgate and cab as he sped from the parking lot and fishtailed onto the frontage road adjacent to the motel. Glass shattered from the back, sending tiny diamond-like fragments into the front seat. Case grabbed Trevor by the collar, shoved him into the floorboard, and glanced back in the rear-view mirror. The tattooed man just stood there beside the bleeding body of his partner, watching as Case accelerated up the on-ramp to I-81.

"You okay?"

Trevor looked up from the floorboard, his face pale and eyes wide.

"Take a deep breath, buddy. We're clear for now."

Joe watched as the old pickup truck crested the on-ramp and disappeared onto the interstate. He'd been completely focused on stopping Younger until he noticed Augie slumped against the wall beside the door.

"Fuck! Augie." Joe yelled as he shoved the pistol into his waistband and knelt beside his friend.

August knew he wasn't going to survive his wounds, so he grasped at Joe in a desperate attempt to get him to listen. He looked down at the three holes in his chest and shook his head.

"Joe," August choked, "Go."

Joe clutched Augie's bloody hand, willing him to live. "No, Augie. I stay with you. No Marine left behind, right?"

August fought for breath, "Not this time, Joe. I messed this up, but there's still a job to do, and you're the only man who can finish it. You have to go."

Joe felt himself choking up—a feeling he was wholly unaccustomed to. "I can't just leave you here, Augie."

"You have to. Everything is tied to my Mr. White alias. The car, the motel, the rental truck. You're clear." August was struggling now, but he managed to fish the phone from his shirt pocket and handed it to Joe. "Call Whitlock. Go to Greene's. End it there."

Joe watched as the life started to drain from August's eyes. He had seen the look before and knew the man only had seconds to live.

August placed a blood-soaked hand on Joe's shoulder. "I have a confession to make, Joe…my last name isn't really Moody… It's Blonde."

Despite the hurt he was feeling, Joe managed a smile. "Mr. Blonde? Really, Augie—You're making Reservoir Dogs jokes right now?"

Augie smiled back, and with his dying breath, made one last request of his friend, "Take care of DJ for me, okay?"

Chapter 29

Once safely away from the motel, Case relaxed enough to think things through and consider his next move, but his first concern was for Trevor.

"You good?" He asked, looking over at the boy, who sat trembling in the passenger seat.

"Yeah. I'm good." Trevor looked down at his hands, which shook uncontrollably. "That's the second time in two weeks I've had bullets flyin' over my head. Seems like I'd be used to it by now."

Case felt a knot form in the pit of his stomach. He'd chosen this life for himself, and he accepted its consequences. But the repercussions of what had happened in Pikesville were starting to affect the people he loved. The last thing he wanted was for anyone to feel like being shot at was something they needed to get used to. He knew this wasn't the time to dwell on the decisions that had led them to this point, so Case put his guilt aside and focused on helping Trevor understand what was happening.

"It's okay, kid. It's not because you're scared. It's just the adrenaline. Once you stop shaking, you'll probably want to go back to sleep. It's called parasympathetic backlash, and it's perfectly normal, so just let it happen."

Trevor nodded and continued staring at his hands. Case replayed the events of the last couple of days in his head, trying to figure out how these guys were keeping up with him. As he approached the next exit, Case jerked the wheel to the right and got off the interstate as quickly as he could.

Trevor grasped the dashboard. "What's wrong?" he asked.

"They're tracking us."

"How do you know?"

"Because they keep popping up, and they always know exactly where I'm at. The first attempt on the road was meant to look like an accident. The second was a little more direct. I'm pretty sure I just killed one of em', but if they're monitoring our movements, the other guy'll keep coming. We need to search the truck."

Case pulled onto a wide gravel shoulder and jumped from the pickup with his flashlight. Trevor followed, not wanting to be too far from Case. After a few minutes of searching, Case saw the small black box attached to the transmission mount. He pulled it off and slid out from under the truck, handing the box to Trevor.

"Check this out."

Trevor pulled the box open to reveal the source of their problem.

"It's an Air Tag, Case. My buddy Jason just bought one because some guys at school kept stealing and hiding his backpack. That's how they know where we are."

Air tags were new to the market, and Case knew little about them. Most people attached them to their keys or wallets to prevent losing them, but Case remembered seeing something on the news about a man being arrested for using one to stalk his ex.

"Aren't those things supposed to let you know when one's following you?"

"The new ones will, but I don't think they're even out yet. This is a gen one."

Case sometimes despised the rate at which technology was moving, especially when the bad guys got to it first.

"Destroy it, and let's get moving."

It was a simple task, but Case knew the action would help Trevor alleviate some of the stress he was feeling. Trevor threw the small device on the ground and stomped it hard with the heel of his boot, crushing it into pieces.

"Done."

Case nodded his approval. "Good job, kid. How about we don't mention any of this to Sam or Mia until we get home. No sense in keeping them worried while we're away. Are you good with that?"

Trevor knew how Mia would react to him being shot at again and could only imagine how angry Sam would be. "I think that's probably best."

Case smiled. "Good. Now, let's get movin'. We both have work to do."

Chapter 30
Pikesville, Virginia
2001

When Vera died, Tina was devastated. Her visits home had been sporadic at best. Drinking and partying with her college friends had taken center stage in her life, leaving little room for anything else. Her grades had tanked as well, putting her academic future in question. Now, she was back in Pikesville and about to face the consequences of her own poor decisions.

After the funeral, Tina stopped by BG's for a quick drink—nothing crazy, just a shot or two to calm her nerves. When she got home, James was waiting for her on the porch swing. She'd seen him at the graveside service but kept her distance. He didn't smile or stand. He just looked at Tina without saying a word.

"Hey, James."

"It's been a while, Tina."

Tina hung her head, "I know. It's just that I've been so—"

"Don't."

"Don't what?"

"Don't blame your absence on something else. Your mom's been sick for a long time. You knew that, and you chose to stay away."

James was never one to accept bullshit, so Tina took another approach, anger, "She was *my* mom, James. You don't think this affects me?"

James stood and walked calmly to meet Tina on the stairs. "I know it does. The problem is you don't think it affects anyone else. Who do you think's been taking care of your mom since you've been gone, huh? It wasn't you here taking her to her appointments, picking up her meds, or keeping her house clean. It's been me and Dad doin' that. Your mom didn't have anybody else."

"My mom had friends."

"Your mom had acquaintances, Tina. Aside from work, she barely left the yard. You're the only family that woman had, and you just took off."

Tina started to cry.

James saw she was hurting and decided to back off, "I'm sorry, Tina. I really am."

Tina wiped the tears from her face. "It's okay. You're just being honest."

"When do you have to leave?"

"I'm not going back."

James wasn't surprised. Nothing Tina did surprised him anymore. "Why stay now?"

"Because I'm flunking out. They have me on academic suspension, and I feel like leaving New York is the best decision I can make right now. That place isn't good for me."

"So, you're coming back home for good?" James asked with a hint of optimism in his voice.

"Yes, I am, and I'm not leaving again. Pikesville's the only place where I feel like I can be the person I'm supposed to be. I want to be better—I want things to be better for us, James, I really do."

James just nodded and sat with Tina for a while, gazing out over the small yard where she had played as a child. They didn't speak. They didn't have to. Tina knew James would always be there for her no matter what, and she regretted how she'd treated him. But this time things would be different. This time, Tina would show James the love he truly deserved.

It took almost a year, but James and Tina eventually rekindled their romance. James struggled at first. He was appalled when they talked about what she'd been up to in college. James had asked because he needed to know, so she came clean and told him everything about the drinking, the drugs, and the other men. Dimpsey was obviously unhappy about the relationship, but his son seemed to accept things as they were, so he let it go. After another year of dating, James proposed to Tina one Sunday evening on the front porch of his father's home.

Tina was ecstatic, "Yes, James. With all my heart, yes. I will marry you." She said, promising herself that she'd be a good wife to James and a good mother to their future children. It wasn't always easy for her to control such things, but this was one promise Tina intended to keep.

Chapter 31
Present Day

Celia couldn't find Hope anywhere. Tanner was missing too, so she was worried for the girl's safety. Celia rushed hurriedly from room to room, opening and closing doors, when she ran into Ms. Adderley and one of her assistant housemaids cleaning the main floor gallery. Margaret saw the troubled look on Celia's face and immediately stopped what she was doing.

"Ma'am, is everything alright?"

"Um, maybe… Have you seen Hope anywhere? Mr. Greene's intern."

"No, ma'am. I can't say that I have."

"I believe I have, ma'am." The younger housemaid said from the corner, where she was dusting a large, ornate vase.

"Where?"

"She was in the kitchen less than an hour ago."

"Was Mr. Greene with her?"

"No, ma'am. She was alone. But I saw Mr. Greene outside a few minutes ago talking to one of the other maids. He was walking her toward the pool house."

"Who was it?" Margaret urged.

"It was Lucinda."

Celia looked at Margaret, "Did you send Lucinda to clean the pool house?"

Margaret's face flooded with concern, "No. I can assure you that the pool house was spotless. Why would he need Lucinda?"

Ms. Adderley had worked for Mr. Greene for a long time and had some inkling of what kind of man he was. Knowing that one of her employees was alone with him scared her. "Celia, is Lucinda in any danger?"

Celia thought about the years of torment she had endured at the hands of Tanner Greene. She knew that when he was stressed, he tended to take it out on the women closest to him. Now tensions were rising, and Celia didn't want to see anyone else get hurt. It was time to tell these women the truth, but she didn't want to frighten the girl any more than she already was.

"Maybe we should check on her." Celia said, turning to the younger housemaid, "What's your name?"

"It's Brooke, ma'am."

The girl's expression had slipped from cordial to terrified in a heartbeat. "Brooke. This is nothing that we can't handle, okay?"

The girl nodded.

"I need you to do me a favor. Can you please go find Hope and stay with her until we get back?"

"Of course."

As the girl rushed to the kitchen, Celia turned to Margaret. "Lucinda could very well be in danger, Ms. Adderley, but I think you already know that. We should get to the pool house before anything bad happens."

On their way across the back lawn, Celia and Margaret passed the groundskeeper, Walter, and his assistant, Darin.

"Ms. Adderley, is everything okay?" Darin shouted.

Margaret waved the boy off, "Yes, Darin. Everything is fine. Just looking for Mr. Greene."

"He's down at the pool house with Lucinda. They just went inside a few minutes ago."

"Very well, thank you, Darin."

Celia and Margaret rushed past with worried looks on their faces, which didn't go unnoticed by Walter, who stopped what he was doing and walked over to the pile of tools sitting next to the fence. He grabbed a large ax and started toward the pool house behind the two women. "Darin, stay here. I'll be right back."

Tanner stood in front of Lucinda, brushing a hand through her short, auburn hair. The girl was starting to tremble, which only heightened his arousal. He'd been watching her since he'd arrived. She was young and pretty, but more importantly, she gave off an air of innocence, something Tanner couldn't wait to destroy. He needed a new toy. Something to take his mind off things. He jumped when Celia and Ms. Adderley barged through the entrance. Tanner jerked his hand away in obvious annoyance and turned to reprimand the two intruders.

"What in God's name is the—"

Greene stopped short when he saw Walter's large frame fill the doorway. The man didn't say anything. He didn't have to. The wooden-handled ax he had slung over his shoulder was enough to put Tanner in check.

Margaret looked over her shoulder and smiled in relief when she saw Walter there. It gave her courage. "Lucinda, I've been looking everywhere for you. You can't just run off without telling me where you'll be. Deborah needs help with the laundry, and you know we're short-staffed at the moment." Ms. Adderley grabbed the girl by the arm and hurried her away from the pool house. As soon as she was clear, Celia stepped in.

"Mr. Greene, someone was on the phone for you." She lied.

"They didn't leave a name, but it seemed urgent. I thought you should know."

Confused by the speed at which he'd been ambushed, Tanner struggled to compose himself, so he brushed his palms across the front of his shirt as if to straighten it. "Very well. That was probably Senator Whitlock. I'll call him back from the study."

Tanner walked to the door and came face to face with Walter, who stood there silently, blocking the exit. The big man didn't move right away. He stood his ground and stared menacingly at Tanner before slowly stepping aside. Tanner could feel his heart racing as he brushed past and retreated across the lawn without looking back. *What the fuck just happened?*

That evening, Celia met up with Ms. Adderley in private. She needed to speak with her alone.

"How's Lucinda?" Celia asked.

Margaret looked around before answering to make sure no one was listening. "She's a bit flustered, I think. But so is everyone else."

"That's understandable. Where is she now?"

"She's on the first floor with Tanner's intern, Hope."

Celia couldn't keep lying. These girls needed to know the truth. "Margaret, Hope isn't an intern. She's a poor girl from Indiana who was lied to and blackmailed into working for Tanner. Hope fell into the same trap I did years ago, and I will not see her hurt any further by this fucking monster of a man."

Margaret shook her head, "We've always known about Mr. Greene's proclivities toward younger women, but he's never bothered the staff before.

"It's worse than you think, Margaret. Just do me a favor and tell your girls to stay as far away from Tanner as they can until this whole mess is over, okay? He's running from something, and it's starting to stress him out. That's never good for the women around him. But I'll do what I can to keep him at a distance."

Margaret nodded, and the two women parted ways before anyone saw them talking. What used to be a tranquil place of employment was starting to feel more and more like a prison.

Chapter 32

August was dead, but Joe had never been the type to feel sorry for himself. He'd been raised in the Florida foster care system and had survived by understanding that victimhood was a state of mind. He'd learned long ago that success in life was simply a matter of finding something you're good at and applying yourself fully to that thing. Not everyone could be a surgeon or a scientist, but society also relied on people with other, more nefarious skills. August had shown Joe that his niche lay in the precise application of violence, which happened to be a lucrative skill when required by devious men like Senator Whitlock.

Despite how he looked and made his living, Joe lived by a code, a code he wished August himself would have adopted. Joe refused to kill women or children, and he wouldn't allow a target to suffer if it could be avoided. The hits he'd taken in the past were placed on men who clearly deserved what they had coming—or at least that's what he told himself. His feelings about killing a man like Case Younger were mixed, to say the least.

As he sped north on the 81, Joe pulled out Augie's phone and scrolled through the contacts. There were only three numbers in it: his own, someone named Maria, and Senator Whitlock. Joe tapped Whitlock's name and waited for the man to pick up.

"Mr. White. Please tell me this is done."

Joe didn't say anything.

"Mr. White…"

"Mr. White is dead," Joe responded flatly.

"Jesus…Joe?"

"Yes, it is. But not to worry. I'm gonna finish the job."

"What happened?"

Joe wasn't about to explain himself to a crooked politician, so he kept things brief. "We underestimated Younger. He was ready for us. Before August died, he gave me his phone and told me to call you."

"Where are you now?"

"I'm on the I-81 headed north toward McLean, not far behind Younger."

Despite the setback, Whitlock saw a way out of this mess. That's what he was good at, after all—finding opportunities others didn't see. "Okay. Here's what I need you to do. I'm going to text you the address to Mr. Greene's estate in Athens, New York. I'll call ahead, so he'll be expecting you. Younger will be there eventually, and you can finish the job there."

"What about the guys he's linking up with? They'll be coming in hot and heavy."

"I've taken care of that. The FBI's Joint Task Force and the CMP have already been told to stand down. Case won't have the governmental backing he expects, but that won't stop him from going after Greene. You can hit him there with the support of Greene's security team, so the numbers will be in your favor."

"Okay. Send me the address."

Whitlock paused, "There's one more thing, Joe. I'd like to add a secondary target to the deal."

"Who?"

"Once you take care of Younger, I need you to remove Tanner Greene as well."

Joe was used to these little twists when it came to his job. Nothing surprised him anymore. "Isn't that the man we're supposed to be protecting? Why kill Younger if you're just putting Greene down right behind him?"

"I'm the man who's paying you. You're protecting me now, so you do what *I* tell you to do."

It seemed unreasonable to Joe that a man like Case Younger needed to die to protect these clowns. He knew Greene was a pervert and more than likely had dirt on Whitlock. Why else would the Senator want both of them dead?

"You're the boss. But this Case guy is turning out to be more than anyone bargained for, and now you're adding an additional target. So, it's gonna cost ya."

Joe knew he had the upper hand and could almost feel Whitlock's pulse quickening over the phone.

"What did you have in mind?"

"The new price is one mil."

"Jesus! You fucking white trash piece of shit!" Whitlock yelled.

"Hey man, you're more than welcome to shop this out to someone else if you want to. Do you think you have time?"

"Fuck you," Whitlock grumbled. "I'll pay, but once this is done, I never want to hear from you again. Is that understood?"

"That's fine by me. Just send me the fuckin' address." It dawned on Joe that he had no idea how August usually got paid, so he decided to make his own arrangements. "Oh, and Senator."

"What?"

"As soon as this is done, I'm gonna pay you a little visit. Have my cash ready when I get there, or I'll send you off along with the other two. Is *that* understood?"

Before Whitlock could respond, Joe killed the line and threw the phone back into the cup holder. This was it. August's dream of "one last job" had just become his own.

Chapter 33

Case pulled up at the Joint Task Force headquarters building in McLean just after noon. A middle-aged security guard in khakis and a dark blue polo shirt stepped from the tiny guard shack in front of the main gate, looking perturbed by the interruption to his lunch.

"State your business."

"Case Younger for Andre Brown."

After checking their IDs, the man walked around the pickup with a long handheld inspection mirror. Case watched in the rearview as he paused at the tailgate and stared fixedly at the bullet holes and shattered back glass. He didn't question Case or come back with a clever comment. He simply walked into the guard shack and plucked a black telephone from its cradle, while he eyed Case through the murky security-glass window. A few seconds later, the four steel pylons blocking his access to the parking lot descended into the ground, and the guard motioned Case forward. Trevor sat up a little straighter and waved as they passed the checkpoint, excited to finally be one step closer to his mother.

JTF headquarters looked like any other commercial building in the area—a large concrete block slotted top to bottom with narrow tinted glass windows. The flat roof was covered in an array of satellite dishes, antennae, and microwave receivers, giving the entire structure an ominous, Cold War aesthetic. Case pulled around to the parking area designated for CMP personnel and looked for an open spot.

"This is where you work?"

Since leaving the Federal Air Marshal Service, Case had lived off his savings and hadn't given much thought to a new career. He'd been paid handsomely for his last stint with the Critical Missions Project. So, if he did have a place of employment, this was it.

"I've only worked with the CMP once before, but yeah. I suppose it is."

Inside, the place was a hive of activity. More security guards ran metal detectors and x-ray machines in the lobby while suited employees stood patiently in line, sipping their coffees and emptying their pockets into small plastic bins. Matt and Ross appeared immediately, but neither of them looked happy.

"Case, we got a problem," Matt said as the two men shook hands.

"What's wrong?"

"They fuckin' pulled us, man," Ross interrupted.

Case was shocked and a little confused. "What do you mean, 'they pulled us?' Did Andre do this?"

"No. Not Andre. He's just as upset as we are." Matt assured Case. "Word came down from the director this morning that we're to cease and desist on this one. It looks like our man Greene's being protected by someone much higher up the chain than we are."

It took several seconds for Matt and Ross to realize Case wasn't alone.

"Hey, I know this guy," Ross said as he reached over and tossed Trevor's hair.

"It's Trevor, right? What's happening, buddy?"

Trevor grimaced and brushed his hair back down with the palm of his hand.

"Yeah. It turns out I had some unexpected company on my way up." Case said, looking over at Trevor. "I wanted to talk to Andre about maybe helping the kid find his mom. But right now, we have much bigger problems to deal with."

"Bigger problems than being stood down?" Matt asked.

"Well, aside from that. It seems someone wants me out of the picture. There've been two attempts made on my life in the past twenty-four hours."

"Jesus Christ. How?"

"The first was set up to look like an accident. It was a coordinated effort, one spotter relaying my position to a guy driving a moving van who tried to run me off a cliff. I barely got away from that one. The second attack was less subtle. Earlier this morning at a motel outside Christiansburg, the same two guys tried to hit our room. I was able to ambush them. One's dead, but the second made it out alive. I have a feeling we'll see him again."

"Fuck man!" Ross exclaimed. "What's the extent of this guy's reach?"

"I'm not sure. But whoever's protecting Greene also has the ability to stand us down, along with the power to eliminate anybody standing in their way."

"So, what do we do?"

"I'll figure something out." Case said flatly, "For now, I need to talk to the boss. You guys keep Trevor out of trouble till I get back."

"Will do." Ross responded enthusiastically, putting his arm over Trevor's shoulder, "Come on buddy. Let's go visit Muriel down the hall. She's always got a big bowl of candy on her desk. The good kind too, none of that generic stuff."

As Ross and Trevor headed down the hall, Matt took the opportunity to inquire about the unexpected addition. "So, what's up with the kid?"

"His mom left when he was little. She ran off after the boy's dad died and got tangled up with the Dead Rebels Motorcycle Club."

"Shit man. That's harsh."

"Tell me about it. But before he was killed, JC Wilks told Trevor he knew where his mom was."

"You think he was telling the truth?"

"Who knows? I think he was just using Trevor to keep himself alive."

"Now the boy's on a mission to find his mom?"

"Pretty much. His grandpa will be here later today. I was hoping maybe Andre could free up a couple of guys to look into it and track her down."

Matt nodded. "He may not look like it, but Andre has a soft spot for kids. I'm sure he'll help out any way he can. But we have to do something about this Greene issue. I put a lot of work into this, Case. We have the man cornered, and I don't like being sidelined before the job is done."

Case slapped Matt on the shoulder. "Do you remember what I told you when we got caught up in that Paris riot?"

"Yeah. Stay to the edges. Move with the crowd and get the fuck out as soon as you see an opening."

Case nodded. "The same applies here. We know where we need to be. So, let's not draw any attention to ourselves. I'll talk to Andre, and we'll get the hell out of here as soon as we can."

Matt just nodded. He knew Case well enough to know nothing would stop him from getting to Greene. The question was, how many rules would he break to get there?

The door to Andre Brown's office was open, so Case knocked on the frame and waited until Andre acknowledged him. The man was large and lean, with a scarred face and a missing eye—injuries he'd sustained as a Secret Service agent protecting the president from sniper fire.

Most people were intimidated by Andre, but not Case.

"Case, it's good to see you again. Come on in and have a seat," Andre said as he motioned toward one of the hard plastic chairs in front of his desk.

Case did as he was instructed.

Andre leaned back in his chair. "I'm assuming Matt and Ross filled you in on what's happening with the Greene case."

"They did. Any idea as to why we've been pulled back?"

Andre folded his big hands and peered across the desk at Case with his one good eye. "Not at the moment. But I'm still digging."

Case remained silent.

"I hear you showed up with a kid?"

A look of surprise spread across Case's face, "How the hell do you know that already? We just walked in the door."

"It's my job to know things, Case. The more important question is, why is he here?"

"He stowed away in my truck. I didn't find him until yesterday morning—when someone tried to run me off a cliff."

Andre sat up, "Elaborate."

"Yesterday morning, some guy in a moving truck ran me off the road. I didn't see the driver, but I got a good look at his spotter just before it happened. Whoever that man was had been following me in town before I left home. Then, last night, the same two guys came at me head-on in a motel outside Christiansburg. I got one of em', the spotter I mentioned, but the other one's still out there somewhere."

Andre stayed quiet. He didn't look surprised or ask any more questions about the attempt on Case's life, so Case decided to move things along. "Anyway, the kid's name is Trevor. He's here because his mother went missing years ago. The guy who led us to Greene told him she was still alive. I was hoping maybe you could pull some strings and look into that for him. His grandpa will be here later to either assist or take the boy home. It's your call."

Andre glanced at the picture of his daughter on the corner of his desk. Despite his intimidating looks, Andre was a good-hearted man and a dedicated father. "I'm sure we can help Trevor out. As for the raid on Greene…" Andre reached into his desk, retrieved two official-looking documents, and slid them across the desk to Case.

"What's this?"

"It's a couple of time off awards. One for Matt. One for Ross—a full five days each. They've worked so hard putting this raid together, I thought the two of them deserved something for their efforts. Since you're here anyway, I figured the three of you could take a little trip together. Just like old times." Andre paused for a beat to emphasize his next point, "I hear upstate New York is nice this time of year."

Case looked at the papers. He understood what Andre was implying and had no intention of spoiling the gift by asking questions. "Yes, sir. Just like old times."

Chapter 34

It was early evening, and Tanner Greene was getting restless. He paced around his office—hands interlocked behind his back, wondering with every step when the door might burst open and a swarm of police officers would take him into custody, or worse. He almost jumped out of his skin when the phone rang. Tanner hurriedly fished the device from his pocket and answered.

"This is Greene."

Senator Whitlock didn't waste time with pleasantries. He had no intention of staying on the phone with Tanner any longer than he needed to. "Okay, Tanner. The CMP has been stood down at the director's command. That should—"

"What about Younger?" Tanner demanded.

"Younger is already in McLean."

"What? Why isn't he dead yet?"

Senator Whitlock took a deep breath. "Younger isn't an easy man to kill, Tanner. The man I have on the job believes it'll be best if he comes to you and waits for Younger there?"

"Why on earth would I allow that? I don't want Younger anywhere near me."

"You'll allow it because that's what it'll take to get the job done. The man I'm sending to you is a professional. I only know him by his first name, Joe, but he'll be there this afternoon, and things will go a lot smoother if you just do what he says. Any action Younger takes against you will be unsanctioned and look like an attempt on your life. Joe will take care of Younger, and you'll walk away to assume business as usual."

Tanner knew Whitlock's main concern would be to look out for himself, and he didn't care for this new development, especially since he didn't know who this "Joe" person was. Tanner felt like he was losing control, and didn't like it.

"Very well. Send your man. But I don't want him interfering with me or any of my business here. He has one job—eliminate Case Younger. If I so much as think he's here for anything else, your little sex tape will be blasted out to every news outlet in the country. Understood?"

Whitlock ignored the threat. "Of course, Tanner. Joe knows exactly what he needs to do. It'll all be over soon."

"Good," Tanner said before hanging up the phone and walking over to the big picture windows that faced the Hudson. His two Dobermans, Bruno and Silas, stalked across the back lawn past the boathouse—alert and observant. *Those two animals are more competent than my entire security staff,* Tanner thought to himself. He didn't like feeling so isolated and helpless. Even though the CMP was stood down, he still needed someone he could trust to keep an eye on this man named Joe. Tanner hit the intercom button.

"Sanji. I need to see you in my office right away."

It was getting late, and Tanner had just finished his evening swim. He climbed from the crystal-clear water and wrapped himself in a plush white robe, then walked back to the rear entrance to meet Sanji.

"Any word from this guy Joe, yet."

"Not yet, sir. No one has been through the gate all day."

The frustration on Tanner's face was evident. He abhorred

tardiness unless, of course, he was the one making people wait. "Well, keep me posted. I want to know as soon as he gets here."

"Yes, sir," Sanji responded, "I'll inform you as soon as he arrives."

Tanner grabbed an extra towel from the young housemaid who stood by the big double doors and proceeded into the house via the downstairs rec room and then up to his third-floor office. He was toweling off his hair when he walked into the room. It wasn't until he looked up that he saw someone sitting at his desk. Tanner panicked and was about to scream for help when the skinny, tattooed man sitting in his tufted leather chair put a finger to his lips. The man nodded toward the pistol he had sitting on the desk and swung Tanner's laptop around so he could see it—a series of video thumbnails labeled by name and date were displayed across the screen. The man had somehow accessed Tanner's insurance folder.

"You're a sneaky little fucker aren't ya Tanner? Is this who I think it is?" The tattooed man asked as he clicked on one of the thumbnails and smiled. It was Senator Whitlock's video.

"Who are you, and how the hell did you get into my office?" Tanner demanded.

"Oh, I think you know who I am, Tanner."

Greene bristled at the familiar manner in which the man addressed him.

"The more important question is, where is your security team, and how could I so easily access your office and computer? You should really consider changing that password, by the way. *Billionaire* seems a little on the nose, don't ya think?"

Greene's face shook with rage. "Who the fuck do you think you are? I'll have you…"

Joe stood up abruptly and walked around the desk. He was

tall and intimidating, with dark, deadly eyes and a facial tattoo that seemed designed to purposely torment Tanner—*repent.* Greene stumbled back a step when the intruder extended his hand. "I'm Joe. I'll be crashing here for a few days, but you should know that already."

Tanner looked at the man's hand but didn't touch it.

Joe shrugged. "Fine. Suit yourself." He said before returning to the chair and kicking his big, dirty work boots onto the immaculate cherry-wood desk. "So, here's how I see it, Tanner. Case Younger is on his way here to haul your ass in. The only thing that can keep him from doing that is me."

"I have securi—"

"What?" Joe interrupted, "You have security? The same security that stopped me from waltzing straight into your little porn palace here? Is that who you think will save you from a man like Younger?"

Greene didn't speak.

"Here's how this is going to go, Tanner. I'm going to stay here until I take care of your Case Younger issue. I don't know when he'll be here or whether or not he'll be alone, but until I do, you're going to do everything I tell you to do. You understand that, don't you?"

Tanner nodded.

Joe enjoyed watching the little man squirm. It was good for men like Tanner to be humiliated from time to time. "Good. Now, if you wouldn't mind, it's been a super long day. I could use a little something to eat." Joe said as he spun the laptop back around and tapped at the keyboard.

Tanner looked around nervously, "I'll call on Ms. Adderley to bring you—"

"No," Joe said. He spoke quietly, but something in his tone

made Greene take another step back. "You'll do it yourself. I don't see a reason to bother the good people who work here anymore than you already have, do you?"

Greene felt himself begin to tremble and backed into the hallway.

"No, of cour—." His voice cracked slightly, so he cleared his throat and continued, "Of course not." Tanner finished.

"Oh, and don't tell anyone else I'm in the house. I'd like to keep the element of surprise, if you know what I mean. And be sure to close the door on your way out, would ya? We wouldn't want anyone else to see these." Joe said as he casually settled back in the big leather chair and clicked on another thumbnail.

Chapter 35

For the second time that day, a dirty old pickup truck pulled into the security checkpoint at the Joint Task Force headquarters building in McLean. This one wasn't shot full of bullet holes like the last one, and behind the wheel sat a burly, old gentleman who gave even the hard-nosed guard at the gate the impression he wasn't one to be messed with. After a brief inspection, the old man was handed a visitor's pass and waved through the gate. He backed his truck into a vacant spot with the word *Visitor* painted between its lines, then got out and walked toward the blocky, gray building, where he found Case and Trevor waiting patiently by the covered glass entryway.

Case was the first to speak, "Dimpsey, it's good to see ya. How was the drive."

"You know I don't care to go any farther than town, but here I am," Dimpsey said as his eyes locked onto Trevor, who stood beside Case with his head hung low. "You okay?"

Trevor nodded, unsure of what to say, but thankful that his grandfather was here for him once again.

"Don't you ever do this to me again, Trevor. You're practically a man now. If you need help with something this big, you speak up. Ya got me?"

Trevor pulled his shoulders back a little, "I will, Grandpa. I'm glad you're here."

Dimpsey's stern face finally broke into an almost imperceptible smile, "Me too." He said as he patted Trevor on the shoulder. "Now, let's get in here and get to work. I don't wanna be this far north any longer than I have to."

After a brief reunion with Matt and Ross, Case escorted the old warfighter and his grandson to the head office.

Andre met the trio at the door. "You must be Dimpsey Campbell," the one-eyed man said as he extended his hand, "I'm Andre Brown, head of the Critical Missions Project here in McLean. I've heard a lot about you."

"I've heard my fair share about you as well. And I want to thank you for allowing your boys to come down and assist in Pikesville. God knows where we'd be right now if they hadn't been there to help out."

"They're good men. And they'd go to hell and back for this one here," Andre said, tilting his head toward Case. Then he looked at Trevor, "I understand I'll be helping you out with a missing persons case while those three are away on a little business of their own?"

"Yes, sir. That's what I was hoping."

Andre stared intently at Trevor. His damaged eye and facial scarring contrasted sharply with his dark brown skin, giving him a sinister appearance. But Trevor didn't look away. Andre smiled. Not many people could hold his gaze for more than a few seconds, but this kid didn't flinch. It showed courage, a trait that Andre could appreciate. "Okay, Trevor. Come on inside and tell me about your mom."

Dimpsey and Trevor sat in the two hard plastic chairs in front of Andre's desk while Case stood silently in the corner. Andre took his seat behind the desk and slid a thin file toward Trevor.

"Case gave me a brief rundown of what happened. Here's what I was able to find so far on Tina Scott."

Trevor picked the file up and opened it. A picture of his mom was in the upper left-hand corner of the first page. It was a mug shot.

"That was taken before your mom and dad were married. She got busted in college for possession. She'd already had a few misdemeanors at that point. She didn't pull any time, but she was kicked out of school and went back home to Pikesville after that."

Trevor looked over at Dimpsey, who shook his head. "I told ya, son. Your mom had a past. You might learn more about the woman than you want to."

Trevor finished reading the file and looked up at Andre. "This says place of birth *unknown*."

Andre nodded. "Your grandmother, Vera Scott, moved to Pikesville when your mom was a year old. According to what I could dig up, she told the court clerks she'd lost everything in a house fire in Richmond. She showed up in Cook County with just the clothes on her back and a baby. She did, however, have her birth certificate—Vera Scott—Born September 23rd, 1960, Richmond, Virginia. I think it's pretty safe to assume that's where your mother is from. I pulled what I could find on her, but aside from a few close calls with the law, nothing looked out of the ordinary. Do you want to tell me what led to her disappearance?"

Trevor could feel a pit forming in the center of his stomach. "I was still little. I don't remember much about—"

"My son James, Tina's husband, died in a logging accident when Trevor was young," Dimpsey cut in. "Shortly before that, Tina had been running around with a guy named Rex Kelley. She left with him right after the funeral, and no one's seen her since."

Andre looked back and forth between Trevor and his grandfather, "I see. Do you have any idea where they may have gone?"

"Rex might've taken her to Richmond. But he came back to Pikesville without her." Dimpsey continued.

"Did anyone ever talk to Rex about it?"

Dimpsey hung his head. This was the part he'd been avoiding, but it was time to be honest about it—for Trevor, "Months before James died, Tina started acting strange. She stayed gone a lot and left Trevor with me more and more often while James was working. Every time I saw her, she had some story about why she needed the extra help, but I always figured she was out fooling around with Rex. When she didn't come back after the funeral, I didn't ask any questions. I figured the boy was better off without her." Dimpsey turned toward his grandson. "I'm sorry, Trevor."

Andre looked from Dimpsey to Trevor. He could see Trevor was struggling with his emotions, and knew this was hard for both of them. "Okay." He said as he leaned back behind his desk, "I have a couple of people I can put to work on this. I'm going to send you three on to the Hilton down the street, along with a security detail."

"Why the security?" Dimpsey asked.

Andre looked up at Case, "Oh, that's more for him than you. But I'm sure Case won't be in town much longer. He has his own thing to attend to. I'll let you know once I have a lead on Tina's last known location. Until then, just sit tight."

Dimpsey and Trevor both stood and shook Andre's hand. Once they were back in the hallway, Case felt free to speak with Andre alone.

"I appreciate this, Boss. Those two are family to me."

Andre knew Case didn't have many blood relatives left, so

the people he chose to let into his life were important to him. "Tracking this woman down shouldn't take that long. I'll keep an eye on your friends while you're away, and we'll get this done."

"Thanks all the same." Case said as he started toward the door.

Andre nodded and turned his attention back to the files on his desk. "You have five days, Younger. Make 'em count."

Chapter 36

That evening, Case and Dimpsey sat in a dark corner of the hotel bar with Matt and Ross, discussing their plans while Trevor walked circles in the lobby, talking to Mia on his cellphone. A six-person, low-vis security team positioned themselves in and around the ground floor, on alert for the tattooed man Case had described to Andre. Everyone was on edge. Case knew that if Tanner Greene went free, Pikesville would still be in his crosshairs. Based on what they knew of the man, he wouldn't be the type to just cut his losses and walk away.

Dimpsey had his own set of troubles. He was terrified of what Trevor might discover about his mother and how it might affect him. He didn't want the boy to suffer any more than he already had. With tensions high and plenty of unknowns on the horizon, the best anyone could do for tonight was to have a drink and try to relax. Ross walked to the bar and returned with three lowball glasses filled to the brim with Buffalo Trace bourbon whiskey.

"Here ya go, boys. Drink up."

"Hell fire, you fellas pour 'em deep, don't ya?" Dimpsey said as he grabbed his glass and took a long, slow pull. He swallowed hard, then set his glass back on the table and wiped at his mouth. "So, you three will leave in the morning?"

"Yeah," Matt answered, "I rented a small house in Athens, New York, just off Water Street. That'll be our base of operations. Andre was also kind enough to let us check out some equipment, so once we get there, we can start on the reconnaissance right away. We already have a lot of intel from the observation teams that had eyes on the place before we got pulled off. We also have the floor plans and survey maps for Greene's estate. We'll drive two POVs to the target site. We don't know if Greene has security spread throughout town, so it's best if we keep a low profile. And it's always good to have an extra set of wheels just to be on the safe side."

Ross sat up on the edge of his chair. "The intel we have so far indicates that Greene has a four-man security detail on site. If they're half as incompetent as the ones we ran into in Pikesville, they shouldn't be a problem."

"Let's hope so." Case agreed.

"Tanner also has a few of his employees with him and a small contingent of house staff." Matt added, "We have no way of knowing where their allegiances lie, so we'll have to be cautious. Plus, we still have the tattooed man to contend with. God knows where he'll pop up next."

"What you don't know can definitely kill you," Ross muttered as Trevor walked back into the room and joined the others.

"Everything good back home, buddy?" Case asked.

"Yeah. Mia says hi, and for you to be sure to call Sam. And they've been mindin' the cattle, Grandpa. They said not to worry about anything. They have it all under control till we get back."

Dimpsey nodded and patted Trevor lovingly on the back. "Those are two good women. You boys are lucky to have 'em."

"They're certainly worth getting back home to," Case added. "But until then, I say we just try to relax and enjoy our night together. We start fresh in the morning."

Matt and Ross raised their glasses in agreement. Case and

Dimpsey joined in with Trevor, who added a freshly opened bottle of Dr. Pepper to the mix.

"Till Valhalla, my brothers," Ross toasted. "This one's for the warfighters."

Case looked over at Trevor, who seemed enthralled by the camaraderie he felt at the table. The boy had been through more violence and uncertainty in the past couple of weeks than most people would suffer in a lifetime. Still, he sat there with a table full of combat-hardened veterans, ready to hold his own against whatever came next. "To the warfighters," Case echoed, "The old…and the new."

Chapter 37
Pikesville, Virginia
2002

Winter was finally over, and everywhere James looked, he could see wildflowers. The bright blues and yellows of spring dotted the hills and valleys surrounding Pikesville like little splashes of color across a vast canvas of green. But right now, the only flowers James could see were the ones Tina carried down the aisle.

James couldn't take his eyes off the woman he was about to marry. Old man Browder played "Canon in D" on the violin his great-grandfather had brought over from Germany as Tina stepped slowly through the small crowd and took her place under the arbor Dimpsey had built for them. Friends and family sat in folding chairs, smiling contentedly as the happy couple faced each other, signaling Pastor Horton to begin.

The wedding ceremony was short and sweet. When it was over, James felt happier than he had in ages. The newlyweds shared their first kiss as a married couple and retreated into the barn, which Dimpsey had set up for the reception. A small group of young women immediately surrounded Tina, each wanting to be the first to congratulate her on the happy occasion. That gave James a little time to speak with his father alone.

Dimpsey stood in the back, propped against a stack of hay bales, enjoying the scene. "Hey, Dad."

"How are ya, son?"

"I'm good."

"Happy?" Dimpsey asked.

James looked across the hay-strewn floor as Tina turned away from her small group of friends and tossed the bouquet of wildflowers over her shoulder. A few shouts of excitement accompanied a clamor of action before Tina's friend Natalie emerged victorious, waving the mangled arrangement above her head. "I am Dad. I think I'm as happy as I've ever been."

Dimpsey turned to face his son, "That's all that matters to me, James. But you have to understand that this isn't always gonna be easy. Tina, there is a bit of a free spirit. Make sure you let her know that she's loved and appreciated. Then, when times get tough, and believe me, son, they will, she'll know she has a strong man to lean on. I don't think she's ever had that in her life." Dimpsey patted his son on the back, "But I know you are the kind of man to provide that for her."

James hugged his father, "Thanks, Dad. I know you weren't exactly excited about all this, but it means a lot to have your support."

Dimpsey just smiled. He knew that, like in any marriage, there would be hard times to come. He just hoped that, for James's sake, they didn't hit as hard as he thought they might.

Less than six months after the wedding, Tina announced she was pregnant. James was ecstatic and only a fraction more thrilled than Dimpsey. The old man just wished his wife, Janet, were still around to see their son become a father. Eight months later, Tina gave birth to a beautiful baby boy with a head full of thick brown hair. In the hospital, she handed the sleeping infant over to Dimpsey and told him that she'd be honored if he picked the name. With tears rolling down his cheeks, Dimpsey held the tiny boy in his massive, calloused hands and gazed protectively at his grandson.

"If it suits you, Tina, I'd like to name the boy after my daddy.

Tina choked back tears of her own and reached for James's hand, "I'd love that more than anything."

Dimpsey wiped his eyes and kissed the sleeping baby softly on his forehead.

"Hello, Trevor. Welcome home."

After the baby was born, life became a bit more complicated. To help with the finances, Tina had started working at the bank, and today was supposed to be her day off, so James had made plans to take her out for dinner. When he walked into the house, he expected to find Tina ready to go, but she was nowhere in sight. James called the bank first to see if she'd been called into work, but she hadn't. So, he called his dad.

"Hey, Dad. I just got home, and Tina ain't around. Have you seen her?"

James could hear Trevor fussing in the background and knew something had to be wrong.

"She stopped by here earlier this morning. She said she needed me to watch Trevor for a while so she could run some errands, but I haven't seen her since."

"Shit!" James exclaimed. "We were supposed to go out tonight. I've got the babysitter on the way over and can't find her anywhere."

Dimpsey inhaled deeply before he spoke again, "Have you thought about checking the bar?"

At first, the suggestion angered James, but sadly, he knew his dad was right. He was aware that Tina had started drinking again after the baby, but thought it was natural for a stressed young mother to find relief in a glass of wine from time to time. However, given her history, there was a chance it could be more than that.

"No, I haven't," James responded dryly. But I suppose I should."

When James walked into BG's, he was stopped at the door by the owner, Samantha Raines. The woman had to be at least eight months pregnant and shot James a look that made it clear she was in no mood for trouble.

"James, I'm gonna need you to stay cool, okay? Tina's been here for a while, and she's pretty drunk."

"Where is she?" James demanded.

Sam motioned over her shoulder to the end of the bar where Tina sat, talking closely to another man.

James stormed across the room, intent on dragging his inebriated wife away from the bar, but when he approached, the man she was talking to stood and stopped James in his tracks.

"Whoa, there, buddy." The man said as he stepped between James and Tina. "You must be the husband?"

The stranger was just shy of six feet tall and heavily muscled, with black hair shaved close on the sides, exposing a cauliflower ear. James was not intimidated. "You're damned right, I'm the husband. Now, do you mind telling me who the hell you are?"

The man took a step closer and stuck out his hand. His knuckles were busted and calloused like those of a bare-knuckle fighter. "It'd be my pleasure," he said, smiling, but his eyes were dead and distant. "The name's Rex, Rex Kelley."

Chapter 38
Present Day

Case sat in the corner of the hotel lobby, sipping at a paper cup full of black coffee. Bright morning sun spilled through the windows of the downstairs lobby. On any other day, it would have been an idyllic morning. The security team Andre had provided still patrolled the area in and around the hotel, mingling seamlessly with the handful of early risers that populated the first-floor dining area. Other than that, the place was quiet. Case decided to take advantage of the moment and call Sam.

Sam was already up and moving when she answered the phone. "Good morning, sunshine. How's it going?"

"We've hit a few speed bumps," Case responded as he threw his chin up and smiled at one of the security personnel walking past. "But nothing that'll stop us from reaching Greene."

"Is Trevor still holding up since the accident?"

"The kid's amazingly calm, considering all that's happened. The only thing on his mind right now is finding his mother."

"That's good to hear. Any leads yet?"

"Andre's on it. Dimpsey and Trevor will meet with him today, and they'll start digging into things."

Sam went silent.

"Are you okay?" Case asked.

"Yeah. I just remember how Tina could be and how things were when she left. I don't want Trevor to get hurt. That's all."

"Me too. But Dimpsey's doing everything he can to prepare Trevor for what they might find. I think the boy just needs some closure at this point."

"Well, I hope he finds it."

Case paused as Dimpsey and Trevor walked into the lobby. "I hope we all do."

Sam wanted this whole ordeal to stop. What started out as one man trying to get rid of a threat to his hometown had snowballed into a governmental push to topple a human trafficking ring at its highest levels. It all had to end somewhere, and she hoped this was it.

"I want you to make me a promise, Case."

Case was hesitant but agreed, "Okay."

"I want you to promise me that once this guy Greene is in cuffs or dead or whatever, this thing you've gotten yourself into stops. I know how you can be, and I need you to tell me that you'll come home to me for good when this is over."

Case felt lost. He knew what he wanted: a quiet life with Sam and Mia, but his anger and frustration toward the people who started this was all-consuming. He felt responsible and determined to see things through to the end.

"I promise I'll come home to you, Sam. You know I want that as badly as you do. We just have to make sure no one ever does something like this again. Not in Pikesville anyway."

"Fair enough. I'm holdin' you to that, ya know."

Case was uncomfortable making promises he didn't know if he could keep. "Hey, look. I have to get going. Dimpsey and Trevor are up now, and I know Matt and Ross will be ready to go soon. I love you, Sam."

Sam sighed into the phone. "I love you too, Case. Please be careful."

"I will, Sweetheart. And I'll see you soon."

Case ended the call and shoved the phone back into his

pocket before walking over to meet Dimpsey and Trevor by the breakfast bar.

"How did everyone sleep?"

"Good, aside from all the snoring," Trevor said as he rolled his eyes toward his grandfather.

Dimpsey chuckled.

Before Case could say anything else, Matt and Ross stepped from the elevator bank and walked over to join the rest of the crew.

"We all good, boys?" Matt asked.

"Ready to go!" Trevor responded, grabbing a bagel and shoving it into his backpack.

"Good." Matt turned to Dimpsey. "To be safe, the security detail will escort you and Trevor back to headquarters. Ross and I will pull the cars around the front to load up. The quicker we get moving, the better."

After saying one final goodbye, Dimpsey and Trevor loaded their things into a big black suburban parked out front and were escorted west toward JTF headquarters. Matt and Ross walked out to the parking lot to retrieve their vehicles, leaving Case alone with his thoughts. Looking over at the stack of equipment boxes and bags he'd been guarding, he thought back to the beginning—to the hijacking of Flight 759 and how that whole incident had led him to this. Case could see the life he wanted now, just over the horizon and slightly out of reach. He was getting closer. He could feel it. Once he'd removed Tanner Greene, he could settle down with Sam and rest easy. But until then, there were other things he needed to focus on.

Matt and Ross walked back into the lobby.

"We're ready to go, boss," Ross announced. "You good?"

Case's eyes went deadly still as he shook off all thoughts of Sam and home. He grabbed one of the big green equipment bags and heaved it over his shoulder. There was no more room for reflection now. There was only the mission.

"Yeah. Let's go finish this."

Part Three
Closure

Chapter 39
Pikesville, Virginia
2004

Blue balloons tied to thin silver streamers hovered overhead as Tina, James, and Dimpsey sang Happy Birthday to Trevor for the very first time. The one-year-old sat up in his highchair, excited by all the fuss, but it was the single flickering candle perched atop the cake Tina carried that held his attention. Tina blew out the candle before Trevor could burn himself, and everyone cheered. The baby looked as if he might cry, but when Tina offered him a taste of the chocolate icing from her finger, Trevor's eyes lit up with excitement, and he attacked the cake with both hands. His lips smacked wildly as a stream of chocolate drool descended slowly from his chin, making Dimpsey laugh so hard he began to cry. Despite the rough patches he and Tina had hit recently, James felt better about their relationship than he had in a long time.

"James, where's the camera?" Tina asked.

"Crap," James grumbled as he ran into the living room to grab the Sony Camcorder. He'd gotten so caught up in the joy of his son's first birthday that he forgot about taping it. As he searched for the camera, James heard a loud noise coming from the street and looked out the window to see two Harley-Davidsons thundering toward the house.

"Tina!" James shouted, "You might want to get in here."

Tina walked into the living room, visibly upset that James still didn't have the camera ready. But when she saw the look on his face and turned to see Rex Kelley leaning his bike onto its kickstand in the driveway, her heart froze.

"Oh my God, James. I'm so sorry. I didn't know that he'd show up here."

James was furious, "I thought I told you I didn't want you hanging around that asshole anymore?"

Tina didn't want to fight, not today. "James, I'm sorry. I just see him at the bank occasionally, and we talk. I mentioned that today was Trevor's birthday, and I guess he decided to stop by. Please don't make a scene. I'll get rid of him, I promise."

"What's the holdup in here?" Dimpsey asked as he walked in carrying the chocolate-smeared baby. "Are ya'll gonna help me—" He stopped short when he heard someone pounding on the door.

James looked over at his dad and shook his head.

Tina opened the door. "Hey, Rex, what's going on? I didn't know you were gonna stop by today," she said as Rex strolled brazenly into the house, followed closely by the big man who'd pulled up with him, "Hello Tubbs."

"Hey, Tina," The big man responded.

James couldn't contain his rage, "You wanna tell me what the hell you're doin' here, Rex?"

Dimpsey handed Trevor to Tina and stood beside his son, eyeing the one they called Tubbs.

"Tina here told me that today was little man's birthday, so I thought I'd stop by and bring him this." Rex reached into his leather jacket and pulled out a tiny package wrapped haphazardly in the remnants of a brown paper bag.

James snatched the gift from Rex and handed it to Tina. She didn't say anything, but her expression suggested she might run away at any moment. "Thanks," he said, staring doggedly at Rex.

Rex chuckled, "What? You're not gonna open it?"

"Oh, for God's sake," Tina muttered as she tore at the paper, exposing a small, flat box. Inside, she found a picture of a man holding a baby who looked about the same age as Trevor. Clearly, the photo had been torn in half. "And who is this?"

"That's me and my dad when I was about this little fella's age," Rex said, pointing at Trevor.

"And why the hell would we want a picture of you and your dad?" James demanded.

"You wouldn't. It's for the baby."

"Why?" Tina asked in a voice that was no more than a whisper.

Rex didn't look at Tina but continued staring back at James, "Because. My dad was a hard man, a fighter, and a provider. Fathers tend to pass things like that along to their sons. I just thought it would be good for little man to see what that looked like."

Dimpsey had had enough. "Okay, you and your friend here have had your fun. You should go now." He said as he snatched the picture from Tina, shoved it back into Rex's hand, and pushed past Tubbs to open the door.

Rex looked down at the picture, then back at the older man and sneered, "Sure, pops. We'll go." Then he turned back to James. "But I'll see you again, my friend."

James wasn't intimidated by the remark and took a step closer, "I'm not your fucking friend."

Tina jumped between James and Rex, still holding the baby, who'd started to cry. "Out. Now, Rex."

Rex backed onto the porch with his eyes trained on James. Once he and Tubbs were outside, Dimpsey slammed the door behind them and turned to Tina. "You mind explaining what the hell that was all about?"

Tina looked from James to Dimpsey. There was so much she wanted to say, but couldn't. These two men had loved her and made her a part of their family. She didn't know how to explain herself, and with no words to make the situation better, Tina turned and ran from the room.

Chapter 40
Present Day

Case and Matt pulled up at the rental house in Athens, New York, with Ross following close behind in his new Ford Raptor. The early summer heat was starting to build, and all three men exited their vehicles looking like they were ready to hit the water. But the kayaks they'd brought along were only for show.

"Ross, grab the MAV from the back and start getting that ready," Matt commanded, "Case and I will unload the gear bags and start setting up inside."

Usually quick with a witty comment, Ross was all business, "On it." He responded as he pulled the Pelican case that held the small surveillance drone from the back of Matt's '86 Bronco and set to work.

Case was already on the stoop with one of the gearboxes, "What's the code to get in?"

Matt checked his phone, "0327."

Once inside, Case immediately swept the house for cameras and listening devices. "We're all clear," he announced as Matt walked in with the rest of the equipment.

The rental house was small—two bedrooms and two baths with a moderate-sized living room and kitchen. It sat between the town's two main streets, across from Patrick's Deli and well away from the prying eyes of other tourists. Matt walked through the house, closing all the blinds, while Case and Ross lugged the rest of their gear into the master bedroom.

Matt returned with his phone out, "We'll all sleep in the spare bedroom. There's a set of bunk beds and a twin in there, so we'll all have a place to crash tonight."

"I call top bunk," Ross shouted from the corner.

"It's all yours," Matt responded, "Let's get this shit put away and ready to go for tomorrow. I'll call Andre to let him know we made it."

Case flipped the latches on one of the Pelican cases and started unloading body armor, "Roger that."

Ross stood and held the assembled drone over his head, "I'm gonna head out back and send the MAV up. We're well within range of the estate, so I'll have some footage of the house and grounds by the time you guys get unpacked."

"Sounds good. Find us three solid entry and egress points and see if you can get an eye on their security. We need to know if anything's changed since the observers got pulled back."

"I'm on it," Ross said as he walked out the back door with the tiny DJI Mavic 3 in his hand.

Case continued dragging bags into the master bedroom and unloading equipment—battle belts, weapons, and radios. There was an aluminum attaché case that contained the target package Matt had put together. Case opened it to see a picture of Tanner Greene clipped to the front of a red folder. His small, arrogant eyes peered back at Case, taunting him. Case could feel his temper rising, so he set the folder down and closed his eyes. After everything that had happened, he wasn't about to let his anger get the better of him now. He needed to stay in control. Matt walked back in the room, shoving his cell phone into his back pocket.

"Okay. Andre's been notified. Once we have Tanner in custody, he'll reach out to his contact with the Staties and have them coordinate with local law enforcement to effect the arrest. By the time the press in on this, we'll be long gone."

"Sounds good. Did he say anything about the issue with Trevor?"

"Not to worry, brother. Andre has a few agents digging into it. They think they may have a lead. You remember that kid you tied up at the Dead Rebels' stash house? You'll be happy to hear he got scared straight, but he also went into hiding shortly after what happened. If they can track him down, he might know something about Trevor's mom."

Case recalled the night he broke into the stash house on Decatur Street—the girls, half-dressed and drugged, scattered across the room like discarded laundry. There was a young man there, maybe twenty years old, a potential recruit for the Dead Rebels. Case came within seconds of executing the boy. He'd nearly let his anger take him too far, and he was glad he'd stopped himself from pulling the trigger. It seemed that decision might now pay off for Trevor.

"Perfect. Now, let's get this gear situated."

That evening, the three men sat at the kitchen table, huddled around a computer screen that displayed the drone footage Ross had gathered.

"So, what are we looking at here?" Case asked.

Ross pointed to the screen and began a rundown of his findings. "The house sits on a fifty-one-acre lot surrounded by an eight-foot security fence. There are two entrances. The main entrance is here on the south side of the property," Ross said, pointing out the main gate, "and another is here on the western edge. It connects to a service road that leads to the staff quarters and supply houses."

Matt pointed to the northwest corner of the image and

referenced it to the map that lay spread across the table. "This area looks pretty heavily wooded. It's well away from the staff quarters and would keep us out of sight of the main house. I say we make entry to the property here."

"That looks good," Case agreed. "Plus, it puts us on the high ground coming in. Once we exit the tree line, we should have a pretty good visual of the house and property."

Ross popped the cap off a yellow highlighter and started drawing on the map. "If we leave here and head north, we can take this service road to where the property intersects public land. There's plenty of hiking and camping in that area. A busted-ass Bronco parked at one of those sites wouldn't draw that much attention."

Matt looked over at Ross. "That was unnecessary."

Ross smirked. "I'm just sayin."

"Focus up, you two," Case snapped, but immediately regretted his tone. He knew Matt and Ross were always on task despite their banter, but this job was personal, which made him edgy. He realized he couldn't let his temper get out of hand, so he took a deep breath and tried to dial things back a bit. "Sorry, guys. Let's just talk about the assault, okay?"

Ross stood and walked to the kitchen counter, where he poured a cup of coffee as if nothing had happened. "We can all jump in Matt's ride and recon the area in the morning. See what's what. I say we assault in the evening once the house staff is out of the way."

Case agreed, "That'll work. Plus, we'll have the sun behind us when we come over the fence. We can hang out at the edge of the tree line and keep watch over everything. We'll make our move once we know Tanner's inside the house."

Case stood and put both hands on the table as he studied

the blueprints of the estate. "I say we all go in together. We'll need to have three-hundred-and-sixty-degree coverage as we move to the house. If we get separated once inside, so be it. We all know what we're doing. We can breach here," Case said, pointing at a set of double doors, "These lead into one of the lower-level bedrooms. I doubt anyone will be lounging around in bed at that time. But if there is, we'll secure them and clear the lower level. Once we make it up here," Case said, pointing at the second-floor drawings, "We can block any egress by the occupants and drive the fight to the upper floor. Whoever's in the house will either have to surrender or make a stand. Based on what we know about these guys, there shouldn't be much of a fight."

"Any sign of the security team?" Matt asked Ross.

"Two guys patrolling the outer perimeter of the house. According to our observation team, there were only four security men total. I saw no reason to believe that's changed."

"This is all great stuff, guys, but there's still one problem," Matt said as he pointed at the footage still playing on the screen.

Case looked over at the computer to see two large Doberman Pinschers running across the lawn in front of the pool. "Okay, what do we do about those?"

"Not to worry, guys." I have a plan for the dogs," Ross said, "They won't be a problem."

"You sure?" Matt asked.

"Trust me."

Matt and Case looked at each other and shrugged.

Case slapped his hands on the table, "Okay, boys. Go over your kit and make sure your shit is situated. I'm gonna run out and find us some food. We'll eat and get some rest. We have a busy day in front of us tomorrow."

Matt and Ross started emptying the rest of the gear bags and unpacking ammo while Case walked down the road toward the more populated portion of Water Street. To anyone watching, he must have looked like a typical Catskill tourist wandering aimlessly through town in search of some local fare, but Case was far from aimless. He was switched on, alert for any signs that the mission may have been compromised and for the tattooed man who was trying to kill him.

Chapter 41

Celia stood on the main floor balcony, looking out over the Hudson. A gentle breeze carried the joyful sounds of laughter from across the river, where a crowd of boats and jet skis dotted the slow-moving waters. Above the merriment and rustling leaves, Celia thought she could hear something else, a faint but steady buzzing. She stepped up to the railing and looked left and right, trying to pinpoint the source of the noise. That's when she saw it—a tiny speck of black hovering above the boathouse. Just as Celia was about to descend the balcony stairs to investigate, Ms. Adderley stepped out from the side exit carrying a stack of clean towels.

"Margaret, could you come over here for a second, please."

"Of course, ma'am. Is everything okay?"

Celia pointed toward the riverbank, "Do you see that? The little black dot floating over the boathouse? What do you make of that?"

Margaret squinted and stretched her neck in the direction Celia was pointing. "Well, it's certainly not a bird," She noted, "Maybe someone's flying a kite on the beach?"

"Maybe."

But then the dot moved. It flew up and over the boathouse toward the service gate, then to the front of the estate and back again. Staying far enough away that it was difficult to track. The two women walked the length of the balcony together, monitoring the small dot's movement as it flew about the property.

"What on earth," Ms. Adderley whispered. She had no

idea what she was looking at. But Celia had figured out what it was—a drone. Recreational drones weren't an uncommon thing to see, but this one was paying particular attention to the Greene estate.

"Ms. Adderley, remember when I told you that if you or your staff were in any danger, I'd let you know."

The older woman turned to Celia. "Of course I do," she said as concern etched itself into the lines of her face.

"I think you know what type of man Mr. Greene is and what he's capable of. He rushed us away from the city because he's hiding. I don't know what he did, but I know he's afraid and that people are coming for him. I think those people are on their way now, and we need to be ready."

Margaret nodded, "What can I do?"

"I need you to find Hope. Send her to me, then let Walter and the rest of your staff know what's happening. But don't let the security team see you. They'll think something's off and tell Tanner."

"Okay, and what about Edwin? He's in the monitor room keeping an eye on the cameras. Should I let him know too?"

"No. Don't say anything to Edwin. I don't trust him, but he'll be safe in there. The only problem is, if he sees anything on the monitors, he'll warn Mr. Greene, and we don't want that."

"I think Walter may be able to help with the cameras."

"Good," Celia said as she stepped closer to Margaret and lowered her voice, "Whatever Tanner's done, it's bad, and things might get worse when whoever's flying that drone shows up."

Margaret shuddered, "This scares me, Celia."

Celia put her hand on the frightened woman's shoulder, "I know you're scared, but I don't know who's coming or what'll happen, so for now, just gather everybody up and have them meet me in the pool house in thirty minutes—quietly—okay?"

"Yes, ma'am. Right away,"

Margaret set the towels she'd been carrying on one of the patio tables and hurried off to find the others. Celia turned back toward the river. The drone was gone. Whoever Tanner had wronged would soon be on their way.

Edwin squirmed in his seat. He'd been cooped up in the monitor room all day and was starting to feel like he'd been forgotten. He'd been about to piss for the last hour but fought hard not to abandon his post. Mr. Greene had threatened to ruin his career and his life if he took his eyes off the monitors or let anyone they didn't know slip onto the estate. There hadn't been much movement lately, mostly just the dogs, so Edwin felt taking a quick break to relieve himself wouldn't cause any problems. He was about to stand and walk away when he noticed Ms. Adderley rushing across the yard on monitor number seven. It was her pace that caught his eye. He tracked her movements as she dropped off the screen and popped up again on monitor eight, talking to the groundskeeper, Walter, and his helper. After a brief but clearly animated conversation, Ms. Adderly and the boy headed off to the staff quarters while Walter hurried across the garden toward the main house. Edwin watched Walter move from one screen to the next, then disappear through the ground-level door that connected to the garage. He searched the monitor bank for any sign of the man, but there was nothing. Then suddenly, everything went blank.

"Oh shit!" Edwin whispered.

"Oh shit, is right."

Edwin jumped when he realized he wasn't alone. He turned

quickly to see a tall, sinister-looking man covered in tattoos leaning casually against the door. "Who…who are you and how did you—"

"Look, pal," The tattooed man said as he walked into the room. "I've already been over this with your boss. All you need to know is that my name is Joe, and I'm in charge now."

The man's presence terrified the boy, "But I didn't see you come through—"

Joe held a hand up. "Look, Edwin. It is Edwin, isn't it?

Edwin was too scared to speak, so he nodded.

Joe moved closer and could see the young man begin to tremble, "Don't worry, Ed. You're not in any trouble, okay? I'm here to help Mr. Greene out with a little problem. Have you seen any of the other security staff around today?"

Edwin shook his head.

"Figures. I'll introduce myself to those incompetent assholes later. Right now, I need you to tell me what that old lady and the groundskeeper are up to." Joe said, pointing at the monitor bank.

Edwin struggled to control himself. "I don't know. I just saw them talking, then they all scattered, and the monitors went out."

Joe stepped closer and put both hands on Edwin's shoulders. He could feel the boy quaking beneath his grip, "That's okay. I'll track them down and find out what's happening."

Joe patted Edwin on the face and said, "Ed, this is all gonna work out just fine," then turned and walked away, leaving Edwin alone, scared, and soaked in his own urine.

Celia paced the length of the pool house, waiting for the others to arrive. It didn't take long. Walter showed up first with his assistant, Darin, followed closely by Ms. Adderly and her staff.

"Okay, good. Did anyone notice you guys coming in here?" Celia asked.

"I don't believe so," Margaret answered. "Now, could you please tell us what's going on? This whole situation is starting to scare the girls."

"You should be scared." Someone said from behind.

Everyone turned to see a menacing, tattooed man standing in the doorway. Walter bravely put himself between the intruder and the rest of the staff. "You don't come one step closer to these women. Do you understand me?" Walter demanded as Darin stepped up beside him.

"Okay, look," The stranger held up his hands. He didn't seem surprised at the gathering, only slightly irritated. "My name is Joe. I know I may not look like it, but I'm here to help. I think by now you all know that your boss is a bit of a fucking pervert, right?"

No one spoke, but the look on a couple of the girls' faces told Joe everything he needed to know. "Yeah, ya'll know what I'm talking about." Joe took a deep breath before continuing, "Well, Tanner has pissed off some very dangerous people, and those people are eventually going to show up here." Joe pointed at Celia, "I know you saw the drone. That's why you called this little meeting, right?"

Celia moved to the front of the group and placed a hand on Walter's shoulder, letting him know everything was okay. "Alright, Joe. Yes, I saw the drone, and yes, I know exactly what kind of man Tanner is. I just don't want to see anyone innocent get hurt. That's why we're all here."

"Fair enough," Joe said. I'm on your side. I'd rather not see anyone innocent get hurt either. Luckily, the men who'll be coming after Tanner are probably what most people would consider to be the good guys in a situation like this, so here's what we're gonna do."

Everyone eyed the tattooed man skeptically.

"You disabled the cameras?" Joe asked, looking at Walter.

The man obviously already knew the answer, so Walter saw no point in lying. "Yes, I did."

"Good. I see you guys left poor Edwin out of your little group session, so I'm assuming he can't be trusted, am I right?"

Hope spoke up from the back, "Edwin is an asshole."

Joe smiled. "Yeah, I get that feeling, too, but trust me, he's just as scared right now as you are. I think we have about twenty-four hours or so before shit gets really crazy around here. It may be best if all of you just stop your plotting and let me handle things. Can you do that?

"Yes, we can," Margaret replied.

"Okay. We don't need Tanner getting suspicious. I'll know when shit's about to go down. Everyone just act normal and go about your business until I tell you otherwise. When the time comes, I'll need everyone out of the way so I can do my job. That way, no one gets hurt. Sound good?"

"What about the protection Mr. Greene brought along?" Celia asked.

Joe smiled, flashing his silver tooth, "I'm Tanner's protection now, so let me worry about his little band of mall cops. As for you, Celia, I may need your help with something later. When it's time, I'll let you know what to do."

Celia nodded, and Joe walked out of the pool house, leaving everyone slightly more confused than before.

Walter took off his cap and wiped tiny beads of sweat from

his forehead. "I don't know whose side that guy's on, but I certainly hope it's ours."

Joe sometimes wished he were more like August, able to ignore the emotional aspects of the job and focus solely on the money, which at this point was substantial. But after viewing Greene's video collection and seeing the faces of those frightened women in the pool house, he struggled with how he should proceed. On the one hand, Joe was only obligated to the person paying him, which was Senator Whitlock. On the other, he knew killing Case Younger would only serve to cover up the heinous acts he'd watched play out on Tanner's computer. That was something Joe wasn't sure he could live with. He'd made copies of what he'd found and stored them on the encrypted flash drive hidden in his pocket. Joe knew that even with Greene gone, a man like Glen Whitlock could still be a problem, but he'd deal with the Senator eventually. As he headed back to the main house, Joe saw Tanner's swarthy head of security, Sanji, walking around the corner. The inept prick didn't even notice the tattooed stranger standing in the middle of the back lawn. Joe just shook his head and continued on to the house. Hopefully, Case Younger would show up soon so he could do his job and rid himself of these rich assholes for good.

Chapter 42

"Where the hell is Ross?" Matt asked with more than a hint of exasperation in his voice, "We need to start packing up."

Ross had mentioned he needed to run a quick errand, but Case didn't feel there was a need to panic. He glanced at the Hamilton field watch on his wrist and noted the time.

"Don't worry. You know Ross can be a little unpredictable, but he's solid. He'll be here."

Matt heard someone pulling into the driveway and looked out the window above the kitchen sink, "Fuck."

"What's wrong?" Case asked, glancing up from the survey map he had spread across the kitchen table.

"Ross is back."

"Good. Then what's the problem?"

"He's not alone."

Case glanced at Matt, and the two rushed from the kitchen onto the front stoop. Ross stepped out of his truck with his hands raised and immediately began to explain himself.

"Okay, guys. Hear me out."

"What the hell, Ross?" Matt demanded. "I know you march to a different beat and all, but this is a little much, even for you."

Case didn't say anything. He just put his hands on the porch railing and smiled. "Why don't you introduce us to your new friend, Ross?"

"Guy's, this is Daisy," Ross said as he reached over the bed of his truck and scrubbed the head of the big brown mutt tied up in the back. Daisy reveled in the attention and licked at Ross's face while her tail swung back and forth, beating rhythmically against the side of the bed. "I just picked her up from a rescue down the street."

"Why, Ross? Why, in God's name, would you rescue a mangy-assed dog just hours before an op?"

"Mangy! Easy with the hate speech, Matt. Daisy's here to help. Ain't ya girl?"

Case tried not to laugh. He'd been around enough animals to know what Ross was planning, "The mutt's in heat, Matt. Ross is gonna use her to draw Greene's Dobermans to the fence for us."

Matt shook his head and watched Ross and Daisy exchange kisses.

"Smart, right?" Ross yelled from the driveway.

"Okay. Once we get the Dobermans to the fence, then what? Won't they just start barking and drawing attention to us?"

Ross smiled as he reached behind his back, removing a pistol that looked like something he'd stolen from the set of a Star Wars movie. "That won't be a problem at all. Daisy here will get the boys to the fence. Then daddy will put them to sleep with the tranquilizer gun he lifted from the nice lady at the rescue, won't he, Daisy?" Ross said as he went back to spoiling the dog mid-sentence.

Matt looked over at Case, who shrugged with a sheepish grin, "It's not a bad idea."

Matt shook his head in resignation. "Okay. But we're not running a damned doggie daycare here. So, get Daisy inside, and let's start getting everything ready to move."

Matt walked back into the house, leaving Case alone on the

stoop. Ross unleashed Daisy from the truck and ran circles in the driveway while the big mutt jumped and pawed at his heels, happy to be in the open air. The carefree scene made Case think of Trevor. He hoped the boy was making some progress in finding his mother, but he was also worried about what Trevor would uncover. Case forced his mind back to the mission at hand. "Okay, you two. In the house. We still have a job to do."

Case, Matt, and Ross pulled up at the campground just as the sun was starting its slow descent toward the horizon. They'd rented a primitive camping site on the farthest edge of the land adjoining Tanner's estate and set up a spacious five-person tent. That would give them the privacy they needed to prepare their gear and go over the plan one final time, well away from the prying eyes of the other campers. The plan was to move undetected to the estate's western edge, where they'd cross over and begin their assault. After setting up their decoy campsite and staging their equipment, the trio slung their loaded daypacks across their backs, snapped a leash onto Daisy's collar, and set off for a long walk through the woods.

It took almost an hour to reach the edge of Tanner's estate. Ross tied Daisy to a nearby tree at the fence and waited. Matt was still skeptical.

"It's a big property, Ross. If the Dobermans are on the other side, they'll be over half a mile away. How are they gonna know she's here?"

Case dropped his pack and pulled the lightweight Crye precision body armor from inside, then retrieved the upper and lower receivers of his MK18 and snapped them together. "Trust me. They'll know."

No sooner had Case finished his sentence, Matt heard a crashing noise approaching them from the other side of the fence. Daisy started whining and hid as the two big Doberman Pinschers burst from the underbrush, jumping and panting at the fence. Ross didn't waste any time. He shot the first dog with a tranquilizer dart, then calmly reloaded the gun and fired again at the second. The dogs yelped and spun in circles, but before they could remove the darts stuck in their hindquarters, both slumped to the ground, fast asleep.

"See," Ross said smiling, "Worked like a charm. That ought to buy us a few hours. But if they wake up early, they'll stay by the fence. I have a couple more darts if we need them on the way out."

Matt finally relented. "Nice job, Ross."

With that, Matt and Ross followed Case's lead and began assembling their kit. Once everyone was set, Ross thanked Daisy for her service, and they all climbed the fence onto Greene's estate. On the other side, Case took the lead. He looked over his shoulder, thankful to have men he could trust at his side. Matt and Ross acknowledged the look as if they could read Case's mind, and all three started quietly through the trees toward the house.

Chapter 43
Pikesville, Virginia
2006

Tina stood behind the teller's counter at the bank, running a jar full of coins through the sorter for Mrs. Berta Shockley. The elderly woman smiled and waited patiently for the last few pennies to work their way through the machine and drop into their respective slots.

"Okay, ma'am. That all adds up to sixty-seven dollars and thirty-eight cents. Would you like that converted to cash?"

"Oh no, dear," Mrs. Shockley responded. "Just put it with the rest of my savings, please."

"Yes, ma'am,"

Tina started clicking away at her keyboard when she heard the electronic chime, letting her know that a new customer had arrived. She looked up to see Rex Kelley strutting across the lobby and taking a place in line behind Mrs. Shockley. He was popping up a lot more often lately, running into her at Walmart or when she and James were out to supper. It was becoming so frequent that James had started questioning her about it.

"Sir, I can help you down here," one of the other tellers announced. But Rex just looked at her without speaking and turned back to Tina.

Tina finished her transaction with Mrs. Shockley and handed the woman her deposit slip. "Thank you, ma'am. Have a wonderful day."

"Oh, you too, dear, and try to stay out of this sun. They say it's gonna be a hot one this summer, and with skin like yours, you'll—"

Rex wasn't about to wait any longer. "Okay, lady," he said as he stepped around Mrs. Shockley. "She said have a wonderful day. You know that means 'fuck off,' right?"

Berta's jaw dropped, and she clutched at her chest. Never in her life had she been spoken to so rudely, and she wasn't sure how to react. With no means to retaliate, Berta simply spun on her heels, head high, and stormed away.

"Jesus Christ, Rex. Do you always have to be such an asshole?" Tina scolded.

Rex shrugged. "What time's your lunch break?"

Tina looked at the big clock that hung in the lobby. "In fifteen minutes, why?"

"We need to talk."

Tina shook her head, "Why, Rex? Why do you insist on showing up and causing so many problems for me and James?"

Tina had been around her fair share of men. She understood how the majority of them operated. They'd say or do whatever was necessary to get what they wanted. Then they'd either make some excuse as to why they couldn't stay or just disappear altogether. Rex, however, was different. He'd been in town for several years now and had always found ways to stay close to Tina, but he had never once put a hand on her or tried to make a move. If she was honest with herself, that was one of the reasons she considered him to be an asshole.

"I'm not trying to cause any problems with you and James. I just want to talk."

"Talk about what, Rex?"

Rex leaned on the counter and slid a small piece of paper across to Tina, "About this."

Tina rolled her eyes and grabbed the paper. There was nothing written on it, so she turned it over. At first, Tina thought it must be some sort of joke. It didn't seem that long ago Rex had shown up at Trevor's first birthday party doing exactly the same thing. Now Trevor was three, and here stood Rex with the same old photograph he'd tried to give her before.

"Why in the hell do you keep trying to give me this, Rex?"

Rex shook his head, "That's not the same picture from before. Just look at it."

The paper was worn and folded with a torn edge on the left-hand side. Just to the right of the tear was a young woman holding a baby in a tiny pink dress. The woman's eyes were sad and distant, and she wasn't smiling. In fact, she looked utterly miserable.

Tina felt as though she couldn't breathe when she realized what she was looking at. She stood, frozen in the moment, unblinking as she struggled to process the shock. "That's my mom, Rex. How the hell did you get this?"

Rex reached into his shirt pocket and came out with another photograph. "This is the one I brought to you at the birthday party."

Tina plucked the second photo from Rex's hand and examined it, realizing they were two halves of the same picture. She placed the torn edges together. Now, the image was complete and unsettling. Rex and his father stood side by side with Tina and her mother—together.

Tina's mouth went dry, and the color drained from her face. She didn't want to believe what she was seeing. "What the fuck," she mumbled.

"That's us, Tina. You're my sister—my twin, and just like that fuckin' picture, our parents tore us apart when we were just babies."

Tina's eyes filled with disbelief. She and Rex looked almost identical in the picture. She looked up at him now and saw something she'd never noticed before. Through the battered brow and scarring, Tina saw traces of her mother—their mother. Rex was telling the truth, but none of it made any sense. How could her mom have let her live her whole life without telling her she had a brother? A twin, no less. Questions poured into Tina's mind faster than she could keep up, "Rex, how…why did…"

"Look, I know you have questions—so did I. So, let's start with this," Rex reached into his back pocket and came out with a letter. The crumpled envelope was opened and addressed to Rex Kelley, care of FCI Beckley, West Virginia. "Our dad, Jack Kelley, passed away when I was locked up, but before he died, he wrote this. It explains everything. I'll be outside when you get your lunch break, okay?"

Tina grasped the letter in both hands without looking up. "I'll meet you out back."

Two women sat at the picnic table behind the bank, smoking cigarettes and enjoying the weather. Both stood and left when Rex walked out and sat beside them.

"Leaving so soon, ladies?"

"You're not exactly pleasant company," Tina said as she came through the back door and sat across the table from Rex.

"Did you read it?" He asked.

Tina nodded and handed the letter back to Rex.

"So?"

Discovering that she had family beyond her mother was overwhelming for Tina. She now knew that her father's name was Jack Kelley and that Rex was her fraternal twin. In the letter, her ailing father explained how his relationship with her mother had ended, taking full responsibility for ripping their family apart. It was a deathbed confession from a tortured soul. Their father also urged his son to find Tina once he was released from prison and to make amends on his behalf. But Tina wasn't ready for the change. It was too much.

"Rex, I don't know what you expect, but we're two very different people. Everyone around here knows what you're up to in that trailer park with your biker friends, and I don't want any part of it."

"What? The Grandview thing? That's just a little side hustle. But I'm working on something big with a man in New York, Tina. Something that could really set us up for life."

"I don't care what you have going on, Rex. I don't need it in my life right now, and I certainly don't need James finding out about this," Tina said as she slid the two halves of the photo across the table to Rex.

"What are you saying?" Rex asked angrily, "I've kept my distance and waited till the time was right. This thing I'm working on up north can make us a lot of money, Tina. We could—"

"Stop." Tina was torn by the revelation that she had a brother, but it didn't change the fact that her life was with James and Trevor now. "This isn't happening. There is no *we*, Rex, I've lived my whole life without you. I don't know you, and you don't know me. I have my own family now, and I won't let you drag them into whatever scheme this is you're runnin'. I need you to leave us alone."

The look on Rex's face turned from concerned to threatening in the blink of an eye, "I'm your fucking brother, Tina. Dad wanted us to be together. You read it yourself."

Tina stood, "He wasn't my father, Rex, and you've been no

brother to me. So, please stop coming around my family and leave me the hell alone."

Tina turned and walked back inside, leaving Rex alone with the letter and old photograph. He looked at them and felt the hate starting to boil inside himself. But hatred for what? His father? Tina? Himself? With no real focal point for his rage, Rex stood and tore the letter and picture into tiny pieces, then tossed them across the parking lot, watching silently as the last remnants of his father's dying wish tumbled away in the breeze.

Chapter 44
Present Day

Matt peered through the Steiner military-marine 7x50 binoculars toward the northwestern corner of Tanner Greene's estate home as Case and Ross covered his flanks. From their position in the tree line, they could see the rear of the house and had a complete view of all three floors, along with the adjacent structures, such as the pool house, boathouse, and staff quarters.

"Any movement?" Ross asked.

I've had eyes on all four of the security guys. It looks like they're all packing pistols. No visible long-range weapons. Two are patrolling the perimeter of the house. The other two have gone inside."

Case moved closer, "And the staff?"

"We know the three employees Greene brought along are still inside. The only house staff I've seen are one of the maids and a groundskeeper. The maid went inside with the rest. I lost visual on the groundskeeper, but he's been staying close to the main house."

Case did the quick math, "So the target has two guards and four presumed noncombatants with him on the inside."

Ross tapped Matt and pointed toward the staff quarters, "Movement."

Matt turned the binoculars toward the staff houses, "Yeah, we got four females dressed in housekeeper garb and one military-aged male. Judging by the way he's dressed, I'd say he's the other groundskeeper."

"What are they doing?" Case asked.

"Nothing. They all just rushed inside and shut the door."

Ross exhaled sharply, "Shit, man. You think they know something's up?"

"I don't know how they would," Case responded. "Maybe after a week of being cooped up with Greene, they all just know to keep their distance. That being said, I don't want to bypass anyone on our way to the main house. We don't need any unknowns showing up behind us unexpectedly."

"So, first stop, rescue the maidens and their young protector?" Ross quipped.

Case got to one knee and scanned the yard for signs of movement, "Sure, Ross. And you can be the shining knight that leads the way."

Ross smiled slyly and checked the chamber of his MK18, "Saddle up, boys."

As the sun started to set, Lucinda and the others stood by the large picture window in the staff quarters' day room, looking out toward the main house. They had been told that whoever was after Tanner would arrive soon. In their minds, they imagined platoons of men in uniforms spilling out of helicopters and storming the property like they'd seen in movies, so they were caught off guard when the door suddenly burst open, and only three men in jeans, t-shirts, and body armor rushed inside, brandishing weapons. No one had seen them coming.

"Everybody down!" One man demanded as he swung his weapon around the room. The other two men peeled off in different directions, repeating the same command, "Everybody down!"

Terrified, they all fell flat on their stomachs with their hands outstretched by their sides, but their fear soon subsided when one of the men spoke again. He was tall and lean, with a deep, commanding voice. But it was the intensity of his fierce blue eyes that demanded everyone's attention.

"You," the blue-eyed man said, pointing at Lucinda. Are you the only ones here?"

"Yes, we are," Lucinda answered with a note of fear in her voice. "We were told to hide here until everything was over."

Lucinda saw the man's shoulders relax, and the other two men lower their weapons.

"Okay. Everybody on your feet,"

Lucinda and the others stood with their hands held high in the air.

"It's okay. Put your hands down." Ross stated, "We're the good guys."

Case walked over to Lucinda and pulled a chair from the small table in the corner. "Here, have a seat and tell us what's happening. Who knew we were coming?" He asked as he took a seat beside the frightened girl.

"Mr. Greene's assistant, Celia, knew that something was happening. She saw a drone yesterday and told us that Mr. Greene was in a lot of trouble and that people would be coming to take him away."

"Does Mr. Greene know about this?" Ross asked from the side of the room.

Lucinda shook her head, "No. Just our staff. And the tattooed man, Joe."

Case looked at Ross, who shrugged. "I never saw a tattooed

man on the drone footage, boss."

"And no one fitting that description was outside the house before we left the tree line," Matt added.

Case turned back to Lucinda, "What did this man tell you?"

"He said he was here to do a job and for us to all stay out of his way. He told us he knew what Tanner was and that he didn't want to see anyone innocent get hurt."

Ross started pacing the room, "So this dude's the one who's been trying to kill you? That could be a big problem, Case. How should we play this?"

Case stood and addressed the small group of workers, "Okay. Listen up. We'll send someone back to let you know once Tanner is in custody and the property's secured. Until then, we need you all to stay away from the main house. Does anyone here have contact with the people inside?"

Lucinda raised her hand, "I have the number of Mr. Greene's assistant, Celia. She's the only one they didn't make turn in her cell phone. I can call her from the landline."

"Okay, good."

"And I have Walter's number," A young man blurted from the corner.

"What's your name, and who's Walter?" Case asked.

"I'm Darin, Walter's the head groundskeeper. He's staying outside, close to the house, to keep an eye on the two security guards who patrol the place. When they took everyone's phone, Walt kept his. It's a big, clunky flip phone, but they never found it."

Case looked over at Matt, who nodded, "We saw him. He's still out there."

Case stood in silence for a while before speaking again. Last-minute adjustments to fluid situations like these were nothing new. He'd learned long ago that even the best-laid plans were nothing more than a point from which to deviate when things went wrong. He just needed to work the problem and find the right solution.

"Okay. Change of plan. Lucinda, I need you to call Celia. Have her gather any staff inside the house and move them to the lower floor. Tell her not to alert Mr. Greene or any of his men." Then, Case turned to the teenage boy in the corner, "Darin, you call Walter and tell him to position himself between us and the house. Have him signal when the roving patrol is on the other side of the property. That's when we'll move. We'll take out the patrol, evacuate the staff, and Walter can escort everyone back here. Then you all stay put until you hear from one of us. Got it?"

Everyone's head bobbed in agreement. As Lucinda and Darin set about their assignments, Case and his team huddled by the door.

Matt brushed his fingers through his now sweat-soaked hair, "Fuck, Case. This tattooed guy doesn't sound like he has any love for Greene, but his presence here is gonna complicate things."

Case understood Matt's concerns, "He's here for me, and I'm not putting you or Ross in this guy's crosshairs, so here's what we're gonna do. We have to neutralize the outside patrol first. Once that's done and we have the staff out, that'll leave Tanner, two more security guards, and our tattooed man on the inside. We know Tanner's protection detail is half-assed at best. You and Ross can get those guys out of the way, and I'll go after Greene alone. I'll deal with this guy they call Joe when the time comes."

"All due respect, Case, but that's not happening." Matt insisted.

Case could see the resolve in his teammate's eyes. There's no way they'd leave him alone in that house with an assassin on the loose.

"Fine. We'll neutralize the security inside. Then link up and go after Greene together, but keep your eyes peeled for the tattooed guy. We need to be cautious. You guys good with that?"

Matt and Ross agreed, and the three men returned to the house staff, "Everyone's clear on what they need to do, right?" Matt asked.

Everyone nodded.

Lucinda hung up the phone and turned to Case, "Celia knows you're coming, but she said she can't leave the house. There's something she has to do for Joe. She told me Ms. Adderley, the head housekeeper, will meet you on the first floor. She'll have everyone standing by downstairs when you make it to the house."

"And Walter said he'd take care of the outside security and meet you around back to let you in," Darin stated confidently.

Case turned, "What did he mean, 'He'll take care of the security? And what the hell does Tanner's assistant need to do for this Joe guy?"

Lucinda and the young man just shrugged.

"Well damn, boys, this just keeps getting better." Ross said from the door, "Looks like we should get moving before Celia and the groundskeeper do our jobs for us."

Case led the way across the back lawn with Matt and Ross following closely behind—weapons shouldered and scanning. When they rounded the corner of the garden, they were met by Walter, who stood next to a small tool shed holding a shovel.

"Walter?" Case asked.

"Yes, sir," The older man responded.

"Where's the outside security? Have you had eyes on them?"

Walter pushed the shovel forward and smiled, "Oh, I've had more than eyes on them."

Ross peeked around the shed to see two unconscious bodies lying next to the house. "He's not fucking around, boss. We got two of Tanner's men down by the back corner."

Case shook his head, "I'd rather you not have taken the risk, but we appreciate your help."

Walter nodded, "Trust me. It was my pleasure."

"Okay, Walter. I need you to wait here until I send the others out to you. Take everyone back to the staff house and watch over things there until we finish what we have to do."

Walter unsnapped the key ring hanging from his belt. "Take these. This one's to the back door," he said as he separated one of the keys from the rest. "The others will open any locked doors you might find inside."

Case took the keys and thanked the man. Walter reassumed his position behind the toolshed and waited while Case and his team secured the two unconscious security guards and moved toward the main house. As the day's last rays of sunlight slipped over the horizon, the three men stacked up on the back door and prepared to make entry.

Case looked over his shoulder at Matt and Ross, "Okay, boys. Let's end this shit."

Chapter 45

Inside the house, the team was met by a silver-haired woman dressed in a plain but well-cut dress. She was obviously in charge. Case waved her forward, but she was scared and reluctant to move.

"Ma'am, it's okay. We're here to get you and your staff to safety."

The woman stepped forward slowly, accompanied by two others—a girl who looked no older than Mia, and a young man in his twenties trying unsuccessfully to hide the large piss stain on the front of his trousers.

Case looked at the girl reassuringly before turning his attention to the older woman. "You're Ms. Adderley?"

"Yes, I am," The woman answered in a shaky voice.

"How many people are in the house?" Case asked.

"Mr. Greene is in the third-floor office with his assistant, Celia."

"There should be two members of his security detail still in the house. Do you know where they are?"

"No, I don't. I'm sorry."

Case put his hand on the woman's shoulder, "It's okay. What about the man with the tattoos? Lucinda told us he was inside as well."

Margaret nodded. "Yes. I haven't seen him for a while, but Joe isn't one of them. He has been nothing but helpful to us."

"I understand that, ma'am. Now, if you would, please. I need you three to go with Walter to the staff quarters. I want you to stay there until you hear back from one of us, okay?"

Margaret nodded again and took Hope by the hand, leading her outside with the terrified young man in tow. Case saw the trio meet Walter by the tool shed and rush off toward the staff quarters. He signaled for Matt and Ross to fall in behind him, and the three men continued on, moving silently down the hallway, weaving in and out of each room until the ground floor was cleared.

With the lower level secure, Case and his team started up the broad spiral staircase that led to the second floor's main gallery. Case peeled right toward the dining room, with Matt and Ross dividing the larger hallway and great room to the right. Case swung his MK18 into the lavishly appointed dining hall. Fifteenth-century tapestries hung from the walls beneath ornate crystal chandeliers. Case cleared the big room and moved back toward the staircase. He caught movement to his left and looked to see Matt dragging the body of one of Tanner's security guards from the hallway into the great room. *One down, three to go*, Case thought as Matt placed the unconscious man on his side and cuffed him before he continued toward the kitchen with Ross at his heels. The odds were in their favor now, but Case wouldn't allow himself to put his friends in any further danger. He knew that with one security guard down, that left one more upstairs, along with Tanner, Celia, and the tattooed man, Joe. Celia wouldn't be a problem, but the other three could be. Either way, this entire mess was his responsibility. He'd be the one to finish it. As Matt and Ross disappeared into the kitchen to clear the rest of the main floor, Case turned back to the stairway and continued upward—alone.

The staircase opened onto the third-floor loft. To the left was the master suite, and to the right, a series of smaller bedrooms. But directly in front of Case stood a set of double doors that led into the study—they were open.

Case rushed forward and through the opening, swinging his weapon to the left, clearing the corner. Then he turned right to face the larger part of the room. There was an eerie quiet. On the far end, another set of double doors led onto a balcony overlooking the river. There were two blind corners on either side of the large desk in the center of the room. Case took a gamble and swung left, realizing immediately that he'd made a grave mistake.

The man hit Case hard from behind, knocking him to the floor. The impact was stunning. As he rolled to his back, trying to catch his breath, a large, dark-complected man jumped on top of him, pinning the MK18 to Case's chest and blocking access to the Glock he had strapped to his right hip. The darkskinned man rained devastating blows down on Case with his right hand. Case struggled to free himself, but the man was strong. As Case fought to block the punches and keep control of the rifle, his father's voice once again whispered from the past—*It's better to have it and not need it than it is to need it and not have it.* Remembering Avis's old pistol, Case reached across his chest and into the Crye Precision vest he wore. His hand touched the cold nickel-plated steel and found the warm textured grip of the .38 Special. Case jerked the revolver free and shoved it forcefully into the chest of his attacker. He pulled the trigger once, then again and again until the man on top of him gave up his fight and rolled to the floor—dead.

As Case got to his feet, he heard footsteps rushing toward him and raised his MK18 toward the door. His head throbbed from the beating, and his vision was still a bit off, but Case could make out the forms of Matt and Ross as they hurried into the room.

"What the fuck, Case? Why didn't you wait for us?" Matt said in an urgent whisper.

Case shook his head, trying to clear it, "We still have Tanner and that Joe guy up here somewhere." He said, pointing back out to the hallway. You two take the bedrooms to the left. I'll hit the master suite."

Ross put a hand on Case's back, "Boss, you sure? You look a little rocked right now."

Case pushed away angrily. He could feel the rage starting to build inside him again, something he usually worked hard to suppress, but it was time to let it go.

Case straightened himself and looked at Ross. There was no denying the ruthless determination in his eyes. "I'll say it one more time. You two take the bedrooms to the left. I'll hit the master suite."

Ross looked over at Matt. Matt knew there would be no arguing with Case at this point. He'd followed the man into danger more times than he cared to remember, and he knew Case needed to finish this his way, or he'd never find peace. Without hesitation, Matt stacked up on the door leading into the hallway. Ross followed suit and squeezed Matt's shoulder. As the two hooked left toward the spare bedrooms, Case readjusted his equipment, shouldered his weapon, and stepped from the office.

Chapter 46
Pikesville, Virginia
2007

James had been running his big thirty-six-inch STIHL chainsaw for the better part of the morning. Sweat poured off his brow as he dragged the brush away from a fallen poplar tree and prepared to cut another ten-foot log. James enjoyed the work. It was tough and rewarding. He already had a load stacked high and wide on his dad's old flatbed truck, which sat a couple of hundred yards away on the hilltop, but he wanted to get a few more trees down and limbed before he left. Once he finished, he'd drive the cut logs to Olan's mill, where they'd be sold for lumber. After a few more cuts with the saw, James's ears were ringing from the noise, but in the distance, he thought he could hear something else, like the distant rumbling of a motorcycle. He didn't give the sound a second thought and continued his work. Once he finished limbing the large poplar, James decided he'd had enough for the day, grabbed his equipment, and headed back to the truck. He settled inside the cab, took a swig of ice-cold water from his Thermos, and cranked the engine. He let it idle until the sputtering motor settled into a steady rhythm, and then James shifted into drive and eased off the hilltop. He had about a quarter mile of steep downhill grade before he could turn onto the flatter ground below, so he eased onto the brake to slow his descent. It took James a moment to realize that the brakes weren't working. He pressed down harder only to find that the brake pedal was already on the floorboard, and the truck still wasn't slowing down. James started to panic. He smashed down hard on the emergency brake with his left foot, but that wasn't working either. With no means of controlling the fully loaded truck, James careened down the hillside, picking up speed, and smashed headlong into a stand of massive red oaks.

At the funeral, Dimpsey was inconsolable. He'd seen plenty of death in his lifetime. He'd lost friends in Vietnam and his wife to breast cancer years ago, but watching his only son being lowered into the cold, damp ground was more than the man could bear. He choked back tears as a row of mourners passed by, offering their heartfelt condolences, but Dimpsey didn't hear a word of it. Tina sat stoically beside him as Trevor fidgeted in her lap, still too young to understand that his father was gone forever. Once the final words were said and the crowd departed, Dimpsey and Tina sat alone by the hillside grave, unwilling to let go of the man they both loved.

Finally, Tina turned Trevor loose to play and knelt beside her grieving father-in-law. "Dimpsey, are you gonna be okay?"

"I'll be fine," the man choked.

"I know I haven't always been the best wife, Dimpsey, but you've treated me like a daughter, and I want you to know that I love you for that."

Dimpsey could tell that something was off. "What's happening, Tina?"

It bothered her that Dimpsey could read her so easily, but there was no sense in wasting the man's time, not on a day like today. Genuine tears ran down her face as she placed her hand on Dimpsey's knee. "I have something I need to do. But please believe me, it's for Trevor. Okay?"

Dimpsey just looked at her.

"I have to leave, Dimpsey? I know the timing isn't right, but I'm gonna need you to keep Trevor for a week or so, could you do that for me?"

Dimpsey was confused. How could any woman talk about packing up and leaving her son on the same day her husband was buried? "What do you mean you have to leave? Why, Tina? Why now? And how the hell is that for Trevor?"

Tina looked at her son, who ran along the hillside chasing an elusive grasshopper, "It's hard to explain, Dimpsey, but there's some things I need to figure out—things that could really change mine and Trevor's lives. I'll only be gone a week or two, then I'll be back, I promise. But I have to leave now."

Dimpsey didn't know what to say. There was no controlling Tina or her impulsive nature, "Whatever you need to do, Tina. I just hope it all works out how you want it to."

Tina turned away, watching Trevor play in the distance, then reached into her handbag and removed a small key.

"I want you to hang onto this for me."

"What is it?" Dimpsey asked as he turned the brass key over in his palm.

"It's to a safety deposit box I have at the bank. I just want you to hang onto it for me while I'm away. Just so I don't lose it."

Dimpsey looked at Tina, "What's in the box?"

"It's all I have left of my past, Dimpsey. It's not much, but if anything were to ever happen to me, I'd want Trevor to have it. Can you just put it somewhere safe for me till I get back?"

Dimpsey nodded.

Tina stood, kissed Dimpsey on his cheek, and walked toward her son. She stopped and lifted Trevor, hugged him tightly, and whispered in his ear. After a moment or two, Tina sat the boy down and watched as he ran back to Dimpsey. Then, she walked down the gravel path to the street, where a black van idled next to the curb. Tina crawled into the passenger seat and closed the door.

Three-year-old Trevor looked up at his grandpa and tugged at his jacket, "Grandpa, can we leave now?"

As the van drove past, Tina waved goodbye, and Dimpsey caught a glimpse of the man in the driver's seat. It was Rex Kelley. Dimpsey picked the child up and held him tight, "Yeah, little buddy. It might just be the two of us for a while, so let's get you home."

Chapter 47
Present Day

Kyle Sutphin sat on a dingy couch in a tiny two-bedroom apartment, playing video games. He'd lived here for the past year, ever since some crazy asshole choked him out and left him on the floor of the Dead Rebels clubhouse for the cops to find. He'd only been a prospect, brought in by his brother, Brian, who had been a fully patched member, gunning for an officer's position with the Fayetteville crew. With all the Richmond officers now dead and the club disbanded, Kyle and Brian gave up the biker life and fled for the safety of their parents' old apartment in Sterling, Virginia. Kyle had started working in construction with his brother. Mostly, all he did was carry big packs of shingles up steep ladders to the roofers or lug heavy cinderblocks back and forth to the masonry workers. It was a physically taxing job, so Kyle preferred to stay in and relax on his days off. Even when someone started ringing the doorbell, Kyle didn't feel like moving.

"Brian! Somebody's at the door," He yelled up the stairs to his brother.

When Brian didn't answer, Kyle paused his video game, hoping that whoever it was would just go away. He could hear the shower running upstairs. Then the doorbell rang again. Irritated by the interruption, Kyle got up and walked to the front door.

When he opened it, he was met by two very large men and a teenager. "Whatever you're sellin', we don't need any." He said flippantly.

But before he could slam the door in their faces, the

scary-looking guy with one eye put his hand out and stopped it from closing. "Kyle, you have two choices right now. You can answer a couple of simple questions for us, or you can get hauled in for your part in the human trafficking operation your boys in the Dead Rebels were running. Your choice."

Kyle eyed the trio suspiciously, "You guys don't look like cops."

"We're not," The older man said, putting his hand on the kid who was with them, "This here's my grandson, Trevor. Several years ago, his mom took off with some of your old crew. We're not looking to get anybody in trouble. We're just trying to track her down."

Kyle looked from the old man to the boy, "Look. I don't know anything about any missing woman. I was just a prospect. They never told me shit."

"Who the fuck are you talking to?" Kyle's brother Brian asked as he walked down the stairs, drying his hair.

"There's some guys here asking about a missing woman."

Brian walked over and eyed the three men at his door, "This about the Rebels?"

"It is," The big one-eyed man answered,

Brian had loved his club. The Fayetteville chapter of the Dead Rebels had nothing to do with the shit going on in Richmond. Still, when word got out about what happened, all five chapters of the club broke apart and scattered to avoid being linked to the conspiracy. Brian had no intention of being drug back in on behalf of a club that didn't even exist anymore.

"Come on in."

After an hour of questioning, Andre, Dimpsey, and Trevor were no closer to finding Tina than they had been when they started. Brian wasn't even in Virginia when the Richmond operation fell, and Kyle had only been with the club for a few months.

"Is there anyone else connected to the club who might have some information on the boy's mother?" Andre asked before leaving.

Brian shook his head, "I don't have any contacts in Richmond, and Kyle here wasn't even patched. I'm sorry, but—"

"Wait," Kyle interrupted, "There might be one person you could talk to, but you won't like what you find if he had to get involved."

"Who?" Trevor demanded.

"There was a bent cop, Donaldson. He worked for the club for years. If a girl got out of line and got locked up or OD'd, he's the guy they'd call. I'm not saying he had anything to do with your mom, but he'd certainly know more than we do."

"Donaldson, huh?" Andre asked.

"Yeah. Richmond PD. He was still there when I left."

Andre looked over at Trevor and saw a glint of hope in the boy's eyes. He nodded to Dimpsey, and the two men thanked Brain and Kyle for their time.

"Okay, Trevor," Andre said, "Looks like our little road trip isn't over yet."

It was only a two-hour drive from Sterling to Richmond. Andre, Dimpsey, and Trevor arrived just after 4:00 p.m. and stood in the sweltering RPD parking lot where Donaldson had agreed to meet them. Andre had called ahead and informed Detective Donaldson of their arrival and what they were looking for. After some back-and-forth and a couple of outright threats, Donaldson had agreed to cooperate as long as whatever they uncovered about Tina Scott wouldn't be used against him in a future case. Dimpsey and Trevor agreed to the arrangement. They just needed to know something—anything about where Trevor's mom had ended up. When Donaldson showed up, he looked tense.

"Okay, let's get this over with." The detective muttered as he looked around the parking lot, "I dug through everything I could find, and there wasn't shit on any Tina Scott, but around the time your mom went missing, there was a Tina Kelley who showed up here with a guy named Rex, same last name."

Donaldson reached into his pocket and pulled out a mug shot. "Is this your mom, kid?"

Trevor wasn't old enough to remember his mom, but he'd seen her pictures in Dimpsey's old photo albums. It was her—in the second mugshot he'd seen this week. Tears gathered in Trevor's eyes, but he forcefully wiped them away.

"Yeah. That's her."

Dimpsey stepped in, "Why was she using his last name? Surely she didn't marry the guy?"

Donaldson pulled a manila folder from his jacket. "No. Tina and Rex were brother and sister—fraternal twins. Born in 1981, their parents never married and separated when they were just babies. One took Rex and the other took Tina."

Dimpsey and Trevor looked on in complete disbelief, unable to speak. Donaldson took their silence as a sign to continue.

"They showed up here, I guess, right after your father died, kid. From what I can tell, Rex put her to work for the club, then went back to Pikesville, thinking she'd be taken care of. She wasn't."

Trevor tried to compose himself. Now was not the time for childish weakness. "What happened to her?"

Donaldson hung his head. "It's not pretty, kid. You sure you wanna dig all this shit up?"

"Stop fucking calling me kid, and tell me what happened."

Dimpsey had never heard Trevor speak that way or seen him so angry, but he felt a sense of pride in how Trevor was handling the awful revelations about his mother. He'd inherited his father's forceful resolve, and it made Dimpsey happy to see it.

"Okay, fine." Donaldson continued, knowing that what he was about to say would devastate the boy. "She served her purpose for a while, tending bar and taking care of the clubhouse, but when Rex didn't come back to Richmond, the club turned on Tina. They got her hooked on heroin and tried to turn her out as a prostitute. She overdosed before she could ever earn a profit on the street. The other girls tried reviving her when they found her, but it was too late. One of the club officers had a couple of probies strip her of anything that could tie her to the club and drop her in a homeless encampment near the James River—just another dead Jane Doe." Donaldson handed Trevor the file. "She was only here for six months before she died. Her ashes are being held at a morgue on Iron Bridge Road about eleven miles from here."

Trevor took the file and fought to keep himself under control. JC Wilks had lied. He'd known all along that Tina was dead and used the woman's name to escape Case. Now, Trevor was glad that his grandfather had killed the man.

"I'm sorry," Donaldson said with a touch of genuine sympathy, "That's everything I know."

Dimpsey and Andre nodded, and with nothing left to say, Detective Donaldson went back inside. The two men waited by the black SUV they'd driven to Richmond, giving Trevor time to process what he'd learned. It was almost impossible for the boy to grasp that the man who'd kidnapped Mia, beaten Sam, and nearly destroyed his life in Pikesville was, in fact, his biological uncle. After a moment, Trevor snapped out of his trance and joined the other two by the Suburban.

"You okay, Trevor?" Dimpsey asked.

"Yeah. At least now I know the truth."

Dimpsey put one big arm around his grandson, "I know it hurts, Trevor. But you handled yourself like a man through every bit of this, and I want you to know that I'm proud of you. Your daddy would be too."

Trevor's lips bent into a forced smile. "Thanks, Grandpa. Let's just go get Mom and take her home where she belongs."

Chapter 48

Matt and Ross proceeded down the long hallway toward the spare bedrooms while Case headed in the opposite direction. The estate's master suite was the only series of rooms left to clear on that side of the house, and Case was certain that's where he'd find Tanner. As he approached the door, Case took a deep breath to clear his head from the beating he'd just taken and sidestepped left, pointing the barrel of his MK18 into the center of the room.

Tanner Greene stood beside a massive four-poster bed with his hands behind his back. He mumbled incoherently through a dirty sock that had been shoved in his mouth, and the soft flesh of his naked torso quaked uncontrollably.

Case could see that Tanner was being used as bait. He couldn't allow himself to get distracted or drawn too far into the room. Keeping his rifle pointed at the center of Greene's chest, Case started giving commands.

"Put your hands where I can see them and move slowly toward me. Now!"

Tanner continued to mumble through the makeshift gag but didn't move. His head shook as he looked down at his feet.

Case glanced down to see Tanner's right leg cuffed to the bed. *Shit!* Before he could move, the tattooed man they called Joe stepped out from the sitting room using Celia Hudson as cover and pointed a pistol at Case.

Case swung his weapon toward Joe, but the man had the drop on him. Case didn't have a shot. His mind flashed through images of Flight 759. The hijacker, Amir Abd Al-Rashid, holding a bloody knife to a flight attendant's throat—his partner, Rebecca, lying dead at the terrorist's feet. There was no way he'd let that happen again. Case steadied himself and raised his rifle.

Joe ducked further behind Celia, "Whoa, there, cowboy. Let's not do anything stupid."

"Let the woman go," Case demanded.

"Okay, okay. Believe it or not, that's exactly what I plan on doing. Celia, here's not in any danger from me. She's just keeping me from getting shot. So, what do you say you and I stop pointing these guns at each other and talk this thing out?"

"Why would I trust you? You've tried to kill me…twice."

"But I'm not trying to kill you now, am I?" Joe said as he lowered the pistol. "Here, I'll even hand the gun to Celia. If I'm any danger to either of you, she can shoot me." The woman took the gun from Joe and held it loosely in her hand. Celia didn't turn on Joe or run for safety but stayed close to her captor. Case saw that Joe was genuinely trying to de-escalate the situation. He still didn't trust the man, so he lowered his muzzle slightly and kept his finger close to the trigger.

"What do you want?"

"First, I want you to radio your boys down the hall and tell them to stay put until we work this out."

Having the upper hand now, Case hit the black push-to-talk button on his vest, "Alpha Two, this is Alpha One. I need you guys to stay put until further notice. How copy?"

There was a long pause over the radio, "Is everything good, Alpha One?"

"All good. I'll notify you when it's safe to move."

"Copy that."

Case released the button and looked coldly at Joe, "Okay, let's talk."

Joe took a small step forward, "You're right. I have been trying to kill you, but the situation has changed. Listen, the hit on you wasn't given to me. It was assigned to a friend of mine—the man you killed outside the motel in Christiansburg."

"And you expect me to believe you don't want some kind of retribution for that?" Case asked.

Joe shook his head. "Despite how I feel about his death, he was also a professional. He knew what he was getting into when he accepted the job. You were supposed to be his last, but instead, it cost him his life. I'm not gonna make the same mistake."

"So, what are you proposing?"

"I'm gonna grab something from my pocket," Joe said, pointing down at his dirty blue jeans. "Don't shoot me,"

"Slowly," Case demanded as he raised the barrel of his MK18 toward Joe.

Joe reached into his jeans pocket and pulled out a small flash drive. "This drive contains everything our friend Tanner here's been using to leverage people into doing his dirty work. There's a lot of incriminating evidence on some pretty powerful people. This one's yours," Joe said as he tossed the tiny device to Case.

Case snatched the flash drive from the air but kept his eyes on Joe.

"You can do whatever you want with that," Joe continued, "You can hand it over to your friends at the CMP and go after all the other depraved assholes in the world, or—and this is just my opinion here—you can hang on to it as protection from any future…problems," Joe said, cocking his head toward Tanner.

"And what happens with you?"

"Oh, don't worry about me. I have a copy for myself. I plan

on collecting my pay and disappearing. The same way you tried to after Flight 759. I know what you're looking for Case—peace—I want the same thing. After tonight, you'll never see or hear from me again. But if you try to come after me, I will finish the job my friend started."

Case considered Joe's proposition, "If you're not here to kill me, then what's the payday for?"

Joe smirked, "For killing Greene."

Tanner quickly turned his attention to Joe, mumbling and shaking his head forcefully, pleading for his life through the dirty sock.

Joe beckoned for Celia to return the gun. "Case, you and I both know the world will be a better place without this worm in it. Let me do my job, and we'll all be free of him." He turned back to Celia, who hadn't moved. "Give me the gun, Celia."

Celia shook with rage. The years of humiliation and abuse revealed themselves in every fiber of her being.

Case was becoming concerned, not for himself, but for Celia. He'd seen this look before—the stony resolve that sets in before taking another person's life—and he understood the kind of damage a decision like that could do to the woman's soul. Celia had been hurt enough.

"Give Joe the gun, Celia." Case said. Trying to coax the woman away from something she couldn't undo, but Celia never took her eyes off Tanner Greene.

The trembling man could sense what was happening and tried to beg for mercy. He dropped to his knees with tears streaming down his face and cried audibly through the sock in his mouth, but Celia was unfazed. "No, Tanner. Not today. Today it's my turn to hurt you."

Case and Joe both watched helplessly as Celia raised the

pistol toward Tanner and pulled the trigger. She didn't know what she was doing, so the first round went low and struck Tanner in the stomach. He screamed wildly and fell to the ground, writhing in pain. Celia didn't know what to expect once she fired the shot. She imagined she'd feel fear, regret, or even remorse, but all she felt right now was a sense of joy as she watched her tormentor squirm on the ground in a growing puddle of blood. As Case stood there in shock, Celia closed the distance to Tanner and shot the man again—this time in the head—then again, and again.

"Fuck!" Case rushed forward and pried the pistol from Celia's grip before she could fire another shot. He then radioed for Matt and Ross to hold their positions. "Alpha One to Alpha Team. Target down. Do not approach. I repeat, do not approach."

A heavy silence hung in the air, followed by a hesitant reply, "Copy that Alpha One. Standing by."

Joe stayed calm and placed his hand on the woman's shoulder. He could feel her body begin to shake almost uncontrollably. "It's okay, Celia. He won't hurt you anymore." Then, he took the pistol from her hand and turned his attention back to Case.

"The person who hired my friend to kill you needed Tanner dead to protect himself," Joe said to Case. "But with Tanner out of the picture, I see no need for this to go any further. I don't hurt you. You don't hurt me. Consider it recompense for your service to kin and country. But I expect to leave here the same way you do, Case—upright."

Case was still trying to process what had just happened. Tanner had met a fitting end at the hands of one of his victims. Joe would disappear to wherever he came from, and Case could finally be free to leave all this behind and settle into the life he wanted with Sam and Mia. If there was a downside to the agreement, Case couldn't find it.

"Okay, Joe. I'm willing to make that deal. But what about everything that's happened here? There's going to be questions."

"Leave that to me and Celia. I know some folks who can come in here and clean up this whole mess. All you have to do is gather your team and walk away."

Case stood there, assessing the whole situation. It may not have happened the way he thought it would, but the head of the snake had finally been removed. He reached up and pressed the button on his vest. "Alpha Two, this is Alpha One. Collapse to the exfil point and stand by. I'll be right behind you."

Joe nodded, and Case looked over at Celia, who smiled. After years of living under the oppressive thumb of Tanner Greene, she was finally free—they all were.

Chapter 49

Maria Estrada hurried to the door with DJ at her heels. She seldom received unannounced company in the afternoons, so it surprised her when someone knocked at eight in the evening. She opened the door to her small third-floor apartment, thinking it must be her mother, notorious for losing her house key, coming home late from her book club again. It took her a moment to adjust to the sight of the strange man with piercings and tattoos on his face. The man startled Maria, but he was quick to put her nerves at ease.

"Hello, ma'am. My name is Joe Seferi. Mr. Moody sent me."

"Oh," Maria said, feeling a little less uneasy, "Is everything okay? I've been keeping August's cat for him, and he hasn't checked in with me for a while."

"Actually, that's why I'm here, ma'am. There's been an accident."

Maria felt her heart sink. "With August? Is he okay?"

"Unfortunately, ma'am, Mr. Moody has passed away. I'm sorry to disturb you this way, but I thought this might be easier in person."

Maria looked stunned, "Yes, of course," she said, opening the door a little wider, "Please, come in."

Joe sat on the living room sofa, sipping the tea Maria had made for him and petting DJ, who had curled herself into a ball on his lap. He'd given Maria a made-up story about August stopping on a lonely roadside in Ohio to help a single mother change a flat tire. That's when he was clipped by a passing car and killed. In Maria's mind, August had died a hero, and that made Joe happy.

"So August was your drill instructor in the Marine Corps?" Maria asked.

"Yes, ma'am."

"Please, call me Maria."

"Okay, Maria." Joe said, smiling, "Augie was a good friend and mentor. I know I look like I've gone off the rails, but I have no idea where I'd be right now if it weren't for him."

"Well, you should never be too quick to judge. You seem like a very nice boy, and I'm glad that we've had a chance to talk."

Joe smiled and sipped his tea. He then placed the delicate cup and saucer on the coffee table and unzipped the backpack he had brought with him.

Joe opened the bag and removed an envelope, handing it to Maria. "Maria, in his will, August left his home and belongings to me. There are a few things I'd like to keep for myself, but as for the house, I have no use for it. I've signed it over to you. I think August would like it if you and your mother moved in instead." DJ stretched and clawed at Joe's leg, "with DJ, of course."

Maria didn't know what to say. "Joe, I couldn't possibly—"

"Maria, please. It would have meant the world to Augie to have you in his life. That's all the man talked about. This is what he would have wanted. Plus, it'll give you and your mother a lot more space and put you closer to work. No more trains or city buses." Joe pressed the envelope into her hands.

Maria felt overwhelmed. It was clear that August had cared

enough about her to discuss their relationship with Joe. Over the years, they had grown close, and she often found herself imagining a life with August, but it still felt like more than she deserved. When Joe stood to leave, Maria walked him to the door and hugged him.

"Thank you so much, Joe. You don't know what this means to me and my family."

"It's what Augie would have wanted, Maria. I'm going to go over there now and grab a few things, but you can move in as soon as you'd like."

Marie looked as if she might cry, "Well, I'll have to save to hire some movers, but—"

"That's what the backpack is for," Joe said, pointing to the chair he'd been sitting in, "And for watching the cat."

Maria looked behind her to see Joe's backpack lying on the floor next to where he had sat. When she turned back around, Joe was gone. She stepped outside the door and searched for him, but he was nowhere to be seen, so she closed the door and walked back to the couch. She nearly fainted when she saw what was in the backpack—stacks of one-hundred-dollar bills, four inches thick, totaling five hundred thousand dollars. It was more money than Maria had ever seen in her life. With no way to express her gratitude to August or Joe, Maria sat on the edge of the sofa and wept.

Joe sat at August's antique French mahogany desk, opened his laptop, and inserted the tiny flash drive he kept on his keychain. He searched through the saved thumbnails for the video he was looking for, then dropped it into an open email window addressed from Mr. White to several major news networks and hit send. He didn't know who'd have the balls to run a story about a disgraced billionaire who managed a human trafficking ring and his douchebag friend, Senator Glen Whitlock, but someone would. Now, all Joe had to do was wait. Augie was pretty smart about not leaving a trail, but just in case, Joe packed up the computer so he could wipe the drive and destroy anything that could lead back to him. Before he left, Joe looked around and spotted the two items he wanted to keep for himself—a framed picture of him and August at his graduation from Marine Special Operations School in Camp Lejeune and a DVD copy of Augie's favorite movie, *Reservoir Dogs*. Joe looked at the photograph for a long time. He'd miss Augie and would never forget what the man had done for him. He imagined his old drill instructor would be happy that his protégée was finally leaving the business behind. Joe tucked the picture and DVD under his arm, took one last look around the room, and left.

Chapter 50

It was dinner time at the Whitlock household. Glen sat at the long glass dining table with his wife, Marlena, and his daughter, Stephanie, who was visiting from college. Members of the house staff hurried about the splendidly decorated room, laying out porcelain serving bowls and topping off wine glasses as the family discussed the recent events in their lives. Glen had just told everyone about his appointment as Chairman of the US Senate Select Committee on Ethics, Stephanie was two years away from graduating Harvard Law School and eager to pursue a career in New York, and Marlena had just finished organizing a fundraiser for the National Coalition Against Domestic Violence, an organization dedicated to helping the more than ten million people who suffer physical abuse from an intimate partner every year. Both women were proud of their work, and Glen was proud of them for their efforts in the public sector. The optics were phenomenal and were likely to give him a significant boost during the next election. Glen couldn't have been happier.

Just as dessert was about to be served, Jordan, Glen's personal assistant, rushed into the room and whispered in Senator Whitlock's ear.

"Is everything alright, dear?" Marlena asked when she saw the color drain from her husband's face.

Glen stood, "Everything's fine, Marlena. I apologize, but I have something I need to attend to." He said as he rushed from the room.

Glen strode down the long white hallway into his office, blindly passing the ornately framed pictures of his wife and child. He closed the door behind him and turned on the TV. The headline scrolling across the bottom of the screen turned his blood to ice.

BREAKING: Sources confirm: Several arrests to be made on Capitol Hill in underage sex scandal. Images of men being dragged from their homes and offices in handcuffs flashed across the screen.

"Jesus Christ," Whitlock muttered to himself. How could this have happened? When Joe picked up his cash, he'd assured Glen that Younger and Tanner Greene were dead and any videos of him had been destroyed. Then he heard the sirens and saw the bright red and blue lights flashing through his office window. "That son of a bitch lied to me."

Marlena burst into the office with Stephanie. "Glen, why are the police here?" she asked before glancing at the television. Her jaw dropped, and her hands instinctively moved to cover her mouth as she looked into the pleading eyes of her husband. "How could you, Glen?" she hissed.

Stephanie screamed when uniformed police officers stormed into the room, trailed by a big, one-eyed man in a windbreaker with the letters CMP printed in bright yellow letters across the back. The man spun Senator Whitlock around and snapped handcuffs around his wrists as he read Glen his rights. Then, as fast as they'd come, the men rushed the Senator out of his home and into the waiting police car parked in the driveway.

Chapter 51

On a hillside outside of Pikesville, Case stood with Sam and Mia as Trevor laid his mother's ashes to rest in the small hole he'd dug next to his father's grave. Dimpsey, stoic as ever, held the ground next to his grandson. Trevor didn't cry or harbor any ill feelings toward his mom. The woman had been the product of a broken home, and although she'd never known why she did the things she did, Trevor knew that her love for him had been genuine and true. The group gathered around the grave once Trevor covered the small urn with dirt and placed the marking stone over top. Each of them said a few kind words about Tina before saying their final goodbyes and making their way back toward the road.

A graveyard evokes memories in its visitors of those who are long past. After saying goodbye to Tina, the small group of mourners strolled over to visit Case's parents, Avis and Molly Younger. Case missed his mom and dad, and even though he and Avis had their differences, he knew everything the man had done in his life had been to protect his two sons and make them stronger.

Their second stop was at the headstone of Mike Moretti. Just weeks ago, Tanner Greene had sent Mike to assist JC Wilks in his plan to kill Case, but the man's ultimate sacrifice had saved both Case and Sam's lives. The freshly installed white marble stone was adorned with a gold Navy SEAL trident that had the words *Forever Faithful* etched deeply beneath it. A gift from Prissy, the woman he'd adored. Case thanked the man silently as he reached over and laced his fingers into Sam's, feeling the thin golden engagement ring on her hand.

Once they were back at the road, Dimpsey approached Case and spoke, "Case, this brings a lot of closure to Trevor. He wouldn't have that if it weren't for you and your team, so I want you to thank them again for me, will ya?"

"I will, Dimpsey, but Trevor deserves the credit. He's the one who set this whole thing in motion. He's gonna be a good man, just like his daddy,"

Dimpsey looked at the ground, still feeling the deep hole left by the unexpected loss of his only son.

"And like his grandpa," Case continued trying to draw Dimpsey back from the past.

Dimpsey reached out and gave Case a handshake that morphed into a hug, then hugged Sam and Mia before turning his attention to Trevor.

"Son, I have something to give you," Dimpsey said as he reached into his pocket and removed a small brass key, which he placed in Trevor's hand.

"What's this?" Trevor asked.

Your mother gave that key to me on the day we buried your dad. I promised her I'd hang onto it and give it to you in case she didn't come back. I think you should have it now. That's what she wanted.

"What's it to?"

"She told me it was to a safety deposit box she had at the bank where she worked. I don't know what's in it, but whatever it is, I hope it helps you find some peace in all this.

Trevor looked at the key and wrapped his arms around Dimpsey. "Thanks, Grandpa. I love you."

"I love you too, son," Dimpsey said, as his voice flooded

with emotion. "Okay. I should get back to the farm. There's work to be done." The old man said in true Dimpsey fashion as he turned toward the road and his old Chevy Silverado.

Trevor turned his attention back to Case, "I really appreciate everything, Case."

"It was my pleasure to help, kid. I'm sorry things didn't work out differently...with your mom."

Trevor hung his head. "It's okay. At least now we have her back in Pikesville, where she belongs."

"Ya know what? I owe you an apology." Case said as he wrapped his arm around Trevor, "I need to stop calling you kid. You handled this situation like a man, and I need to start treating you like one."

Trevor's heart filled with pride, and he stood a little straighter. He reached into his jacket pocket and retrieved a folded piece of paper.

Trevor didn't say anything. He just handed the paper to Case, who opened it and started reading.

"Is this what I think it is?" He asked.

"Yeah. That's my signed paperwork for the Army's Delayed Entry Program. I still have to finish my senior year, but I'll ship off to Fort Benning as soon as I graduate."

Case read the letter silently.

"That's fantastic, Trevor!" Case wrapped the young man in a big hug, "I'm proud of you, buddy. You're going to make an incredible soldier."

Trevor squeezed Case tight, unashamed of the love he felt for his friend. He didn't remember his own father, but since his return, Case had stepped in and, with Dimpsey, had shown Trevor what it meant to be a man. He would make sure he didn't let them down. With the fate of his mother behind him and his sights set on the next big adventure, Trevor helped Mia into the truck, and the two drove off together, leaving Case alone with Sam.

"Well, mister. It looks like it's just gonna be the two of us tonight."

Case took Sam by the hand again and smiled, "I wouldn't have it any other way."

Chapter 52

Mia held Trevor's hand as the two stood side-by-side in the vault room of Pikesville Bank and Trust. They watched as Jane, the bank manager, pulled the large steel box from its place on the wall and set it on a long wooden table in the center of the room.

"Here ya go, sweetie. You take all the time you want. I'll be right outside if you need anything."

Trevor thanked the woman and turned to Mia. "Well. I guess I should just open it, right?"

Mia nodded without speaking, and Trevor slid the small key into the lock and turned it. He opened the box slowly, unsure of what might be inside. What he found was a large, leatherbound family bible, a cardboard box with a fancy floral pattern printed on it, and an envelope. Trevor removed the three items from the safety deposit box and laid them out in front of him. He opened the bible first. In it, the Scott family tree was recorded—five generations of his mother's family that he'd never known about. Mia laid her hands on the pretty floral box and traced the pattern with her fingers.

"Go ahead and open it," Trevor said.

Mia smiled and lifted the lid to expose a delicate twelve-piece tea set with an intricate rose pattern that matched the box. She lifted one of the dainty cups and studied it beneath the fluorescent lights. "It's so pretty."

Lost in his own thoughts, Trevor picked up the envelope. It had one word written across the front, in loopy, girlish lettering—*Trevor.*

Trevor's hands started to shake. Mia noticed his reaction and set the teacup down to place her hand on Trevor's back. "It's from your mom, Trevor. Read it."

Trevor opened the envelope and removed the letter.

My Dearest Trevor,

I don't know at what point in your life this letter might find you, but wherever you are and whatever you're doing, I hope you're happy. I know that if you're reading this, I'm no longer around, but I want you to know that the only reason I ever left was to protect you. There's so much I wish I could have told you, so many things I needed to explain. But that's me Trevor, I feel like I was born running and just never stopped. I know you'll hear things about me as you grow older. Some of it may be true, but I want you to understand that there's a side of me that most people never got to know. When I married your father and had you, I finally saw the life I was meant to live. I was happy with your dad and wanted nothing more than to pass that happiness on to you. To give you a home where you felt protected and loved. But once your father died, a part of me died with him, and I felt myself spiraling into the past I'd worked so hard to escape. I never wanted to hurt you. That's why I left you with Dimpsey. Your grandfather is a pillar of strength, and I know he'll raise you the same way he raised James—to be strong, honest, and forthright. Those are all things I don't know if I could have given you alone. I left so you could be the man you're supposed to be and not be drug through life by a mother who's lost her way. Life is a gift, Trevor, and of all the special gifts I've known, however great or small, to have had you, if only for a little while, was the greatest gift of all. I love you.

—Mom

Trevor folded the letter and stuck it in his pocket. He picked up the Bible his mother had left him and handed Mia the tea set.

"Are you okay?" Mia asked.

Trevor smiled and nodded. "Yeah. I'm okay." He said as he wiped tears from his eyes. "Life's a gift, ya know. Let's go enjoy it."

Epilogue

Fort Benning, Georgia
Three Years Later

Trevor and nineteen other graduates from Ranger School stood at attention in the Hurley Hill Training Area of Fort Benning. After a brief speech by the Commanding General of the Maneuver Center of Excellence, Trevor was called to the front of the formation and presented with the William O. Darby Award, an honor given to the graduating Ranger who was deemed the top distinguished honor graduate and who had demonstrated himself to be a cut above all other Rangers. It was an incredible honor.

Case stood in the crowded bleachers beside Dimpsey, Mia, and his wife, Sam, who all cheered loudly and shouted, "Rangers lead the way," in perfect unison, bringing an almost imperceptible grin to Trevor's lips, but Case saw it.

Case knew his brother Bobby would have wanted to be there to congratulate Trevor, but with his wife Amanda nine months pregnant, they didn't want to take the chance on a road trip to Georgia. Along with the award, Trevor was presented with his Ranger tab and a stone that would be engraved with his name and placed on the walkway to the Ranger memorial, which served to recognize the accomplishments of Rangers throughout the unit's long and distinguished history. After the presentation of awards, family members were released from the bleachers to pin the newly minted Rangers with their tabs. Trevor had requested Case be the one to do the honors.

Pride flooded both their faces as Case placed the arched,

black and gold Ranger tab onto Trevor's left shoulder.

"I'm proud of you, Trevor."

"I couldn't have done this without you, Case."

Case shook the young E-4's hand and slapped him hard on the arm. "This was all you, buddy. Take pride in it."

Trevor smiled and looked down at the stone he still held in his hand. "Do you think they can put mine next to yours?"

Case chuckled, "That would be a hell of a sight now, wouldn't it?"

After the pinning ceremony, Trevor and the rest of the graduates were put back in formation and called to attention to recite the Ranger's creed. Case looked over to see Mia and Dimpsey holding hands and together creating enough tears to fill a canteen. Life as a Ranger was never easy, but Trevor was strong, determined, and selfless. Case knew he had what it took to be a successful leader.

When the ceremony concluded, the new Rangers marched away, and the crowd dispersed. Case looked over to see Andre, Matt, and Ross standing at the edge of the crowd. Ross was holding the leash of his trusty service dog, Daisy, who lay quietly at his feet. "I'll be right back," he said, kissing Sam on the cheek.

"Okay," Sam responded, smiling, "But don't let those guys talk you into leaving with them again."

Case laughed, "Don't worry, baby. Nothin's dragging me away from you."

Case walked over to his friends. They all hugged and congratulated Case on his recent marriage to Sam. After everything that had happened at Bobby and Amanda's wedding, Case had convinced Sam to elope without telling anyone.

"You sure you don't want to come up north and kick in a

few more doors before you head out to pasture?" Ross asked jokingly as he scratched Daisy behind the ear.

Case looked over his shoulder at Sam and Mia. "Fella's, I appreciate the offer, but there's no way in hell I'm leaving that."

"You're making the right choice," Matt added.

"Trevor's honored that you all showed up. He really holds you guys in high esteem.

Andre nodded. "It's always good to see tough young warriors like Trevor come into the fold."

After a few more minutes of catching up, the four men hugged again and went their separate ways. Andre, Matt, and Ross headed back to the parking lot with Daisy. Case looked on as they drove away in a big black Suburban, then made his way back to Sam.

"It's always hard to watch those guys go, isn't it?" Sam said.

Case put an arm around his wife. "It is. But it's a lot easier knowing what I have to come home to."

Sam kissed Case gently on the lips and patted his cheek. "Okay, mister, it's been a long day. Whadda ya say you and I head back to Pikesville?"

Case smiled, "I can't think of anything that would make me happier."

Acknowledgements

The story of Case Younger and his friends is one I've wanted to share for a long time. Growing up as a native of the Blue Ridge Mountains, I was immersed in a culture of storytelling, and I suppose a little of that rubbed off on me, allowing me to tell a tale worth hearing. But there's a lot involved in getting a story from one's imagination onto the page, and I'd be remiss if I didn't thank all the amazing people who helped me along the way.

First and foremost, I want to thank my wife and children, who patiently listened to my ideas and reviewed the numerous drafts of Case Younger's story. Your support and feedback kept me going when I felt like quitting, and I will always be grateful for everything you've done to help bring these books to life.

Thank you to the fantastic team at YMAA Publications: David Ripianzi, Leslie Takao. Barbara Langley, Gene Ching, Tim Comrie, Kristen Miller, and David Silver. You've all started to feel like family to me, and I will always treat you as such.

My deepest gratitude to the International Thriller Writers Organization. Being a part of ITW has been an incredible part of this journey, and I appreciate all that I've learned from you and your supporters.

Thank you to Jude Gerard Prest, CEO of LifeLike Productions Inc., for believing in Case Younger's story and recognizing its potential beyond the written page. I look forward to seeing what this becomes.

To my hometown of Hillsville, Virginia, which serves as the

inspiration for Pikesville. The people and places I mention in these stories have shaped my life in the most positive way imaginable. Thank you.

Many blessings to Cynthia Taylor at Pages Books and Coffee in Mount Airy, North Carolina, for serving as the launch site for the Case Younger Series. You and your team are the absolute best.

Thanks to all my literary heroes: David Morrell, Steven Pressfield, Lee Child, Wilbur Smith, Jack Carr, Elmore Leonard, AJ Quinnell, CJ Box, and many others. The countless hours of escapism you've provided helped me get through many long miles while working as a Federal Air Marshal.

Most importantly, thank you to all the readers out there. Without you, none of this would matter. You are the fuel that drives the entire publishing industry, and your tireless support is greatly appreciated.

Lastly, I want to thank my mom, Reva. She was an avid reader who loved a good story. My greatest hope is that the Case Younger series would have been one of her favorites. I miss you, Mom.

POSTSCRIPT

Although this series is a work of fiction, it touches upon the all too real issue of human trafficking in the United States. Fortunately, you can help. Visit https://www.missingkids.org/home or call 1-800-THE-LOST for more information on how to detect, prevent, and report potential victims of kidnapping and human trafficking.

About the Author

GARY QUESENBERRY Gary Quesenberry is an Army veteran and career Federal Air Marshal with an extensive background in both domestic and foreign counter-terror operations. Gary retired from federal service in 2020 and returned to his hometown of Hillsville, Virginia, in the Blue Ridge Mountains. He is the award-winning author of four nonfiction books on the topics of situational awareness and personal safety: *Spotting Danger Before It Spots You, Spotting Danger Before It Spots Your Kids, Spotting Danger Before It Spots Your Teens,* and *Spotting Danger for Travelers.* Visit him at GaryQuesenberry.com and follow along on Instagram at @gary.quesenberry.

www.ingramcontent.com/pod-product-compliance
Lightning Source LLC
LaVergne TN
LVHW041627060526
838200LV00040B/1476